rhcbooks.com

ISBN 978-0-7364-4030-1

Printed in the United States of America

10 9 8 7 6 5 4 3 2 1

DISNEY
FROZEN II

THE DELUXE
JUNIOR NOVELIZATION
···» SPECIAL EDITION «···

Adapted by David Blaze

Random House 🏠 New York

$\mathfrak{F}$ar away, as far north as any man, woman, or child had ever been, once stood the Enchanted Forest. This beautiful forest was protected by the spirits of air, fire, water, and earth. Among all this beauty dwelled a mysterious people called the Northuldra. They were nomads who lived off the land and followed their reindeer herds wherever they roamed. Because the Northuldra were in harmony with nature, it was thought that they were magical.

One day, ships arrived at the entrance to the fjord south of the Enchanted Forest—wooden ships full of people who were determined to create a home for themselves near the water. Soon the kingdom of Arendelle came to be, and a magnificent castle was built for the royal family.

The newcomers were welcomed by the Northuldra's ruler when he met with their king on a cliff as the sun set. The leaders firmly shook hands, and the meeting was seen by others only in hazy silhouette as they cast great shadows across the land.

To demonstrate their goodwill and friendship, the Arendellians built a mighty dam in the Enchanted Forest. They placed it on the river that flowed into the Arenfjord, the deep blue body of water upon which Arendelle Castle had been built. The dam connected all the lands and made it easier for the Northuldra and their reindeer to roam. King Runeard, the leader of Arendelle, offered it to the Northuldra as a symbol of peace and cooperation between the two groups.

When the dam was complete, the Arendellians threw a great celebration. Northuldra from all over the land gathered at the base of the dam to mingle and feast with the Arendellians. For Prince Agnarr, the young son of King Runeard, it was the farthest from home he had ever been. His eyes danced with wonder and excitement . . . until his father noticed.

King Runeard flicked Agnarr under the chin and gave him a look that the prince knew better than to challenge. He directed his son to stand straight and proud—to be regal.

"Remember, Agnarr—you represent Arendelle." Agnarr obeyed, as the king knew he would. "And mind Lieutenant Mattias," his father advised, motioning to a young man in uniform.

Mattias stood at attention as the king walked away with his guards. The lieutenant knew the disappointment in Agnarr's eyes. It wasn't just that King Runeard had wanted him to act royally, like a diplomat instead of a boy. It was also that he had left Agnarr behind— away from the talk with the elders and the Northuldra leader.

But Mattias knew exactly what to do. He stepped up beside Agnarr and mused, "You're getting taller. Stop that." He nudged the young prince with his elbow. Agnarr smiled and gave him a jab back. "Eh, I'm just kidding. Come on. Let's go." The two interlocked arms, jockeying for position in a friendly wrestling match on their way down to the festivities.

At the heart of the celebration, the Northuldra and the Arendellians intermingled, eating and drinking, talking and laughing as if they were the very best of friends. The

Northuldra even put on a show, demonstrating tricks on the backs of their reindeer.

But something deeper in the forest caught Agnarr's eye. It was so amazing, it couldn't possibly have been real. He thought he saw the silhouette of a girl about his age, spinning up and down in the air as she twirled with the leaves in the wind. She wasn't dangling from trees or clinging to vines, but somehow she floated as if she weighed nothing.

Mesmerized, Agnarr moved toward her. It was only after he heard the clashing of swords, shields, and staffs that the trance he seemed to have been in was broken. He turned and saw that his people were being attacked! The charm and magic of the Northuldra had only been a trick. Agnarr gave the girl one last look, not wanting to believe that the fighting was real. But she was gone—as if she had never been there at all.

The whoosh of an arrow passing Agnarr's head froze him in his spot. He had never been that close to danger before.

"Get behind me," Mattias said, and pulled

Agnarr out of the way just before another arrow zipped by, right where his head had been.

Agnarr was dazed and could only watch as the brutal battle raged before them, arrows flying and shields defending. He froze when he saw his father, sword in hand, facing the Northuldra leader. Mattias held tight to Agnarr as the prince yelled for his father. All he wanted to do was help him.

The prince was able to free himself—but only after the king and the Northuldra leader had plunged over the edge of a cliff.

"Father!" Agnarr roared like a soldier of old and rushed through the battle to get to the cliff's edge and search for his father. But fire erupted before him, and the flames and heat pushed him back.

A massive blast shot across the forest like a shock wave. The Northuldra and Arendellian soldiers ran for their lives as water crashed into the dam with a sound like thunder. The wind began to rage violently while boulders fell from the sky like bombs. One landed at Agnarr's feet, and the force of the impact tossed him through the air. When he hit the ground, his head slammed against a rock. As he began to lose consciousness and his vision faded, he noted sadly that the lush beauty of the forest had been destroyed.

At the same time, he heard a haunting voice, like someone overcome with the grief of centuries, wailing an eerie melody. Agnarr had never experienced anything like it before. The Northuldra had mentioned that the dam was inhabited by the spirits of the people who had built it. *Is that voice a spirit? Is it angry?* Agnarr asked himself.

Somehow, the prince was moved out of the forest by an unseen force that floated him through the air while the chaos continued beneath him. Then the deafening roar fell silent as the angry spirits stopped raging, and a mist, as thick and impenetrable as stone, enveloped the forest, locking some people in and others out. . . .

CHAPTER 1

"And that night, I came home King of Arendelle," King Agnarr said.

The king's candle cast flickering shadows on his face as he told his story to his young daughters, Anna and Elsa. The girls were huddled together on Elsa's bed with their mother, Queen Iduna, listening to every word their father said, their eyes wide and their mouths hanging open. Their mother drew them close to her, all three of them gathered under the comforting weight of her burgundy scarf.

"Whoa, Papa, that was epic," Anna said, collapsing on the bed as she pictured everything that had happened. "Whoever saved you, I love them."

The king smiled at his little girl. "I wish I knew who it was."

"Were the Northuldra really magical?" Elsa wondered aloud. She didn't want to be anything like them. She couldn't imagine hurting her friends. "Like me?"

"No," King Agnarr assured her. "They were not magical. They just enjoyed the magic of the forest."

"What happened to the spirits? What's in the forest now?" Elsa wondered if anyone else had made it out after the spirits had gotten angry and turned on everyone.

"I don't know," King Agnarr replied. "The mist still stands. No one can get in, and no one has come out since."

Queen Iduna locked eyes with her husband, warning him to be careful with his words. She wanted to make sure their daughters didn't feel scared. "So we're safe," she said.

"Yes," King Agnarr agreed. "But the forest could wake again, and we must be prepared for whatever danger it may bring."

Queen Iduna watch a flood of worry wash over Elsa's face at her father's words, and she intervened. "On that note, how about we say good night to your father," she said. Both girls were much too young to think about fighting of any kind . . . especially when she was trying to get them to sleep. King Agnarr stood, and his face held an apology for his wife.

"Aw, but I still have so many questions," Anna said, pouting as her father kissed Elsa on the forehead.

"Save them for another night, Anna," he insisted.

"Urgh," she said in frustration. "You know I don't have that kind of patience." She looked pointedly at Elsa, who nodded, clearly agreeing with Anna about her lack of patience.

Anna closed her mouth tight and scrunched her face. Her father kissed her on the forehead, knowing that was her version of trying. Then he walked out of the room. As soon as the door shut, Anna started in with her questions again.

"Why did the Northuldra attack us, anyway?" she asked her mother. "Who attacks people who give them gifts?"

"Do you think the forest will wake again? What would the spirits think of my magic?" Elsa asked, glancing up at her mother.

A soft look came across Iduna's face as her own memory from the past swept through her mind. "I wish I had the answers. Alas, only Ahtohallan knows."

"Ahto-who-what?" Anna asked.

Queen Iduna laughed as she smiled at the upturned face of her youngest daughter. "When I was little, my mother would sing a song about a special river called Ahtohallan, which was said to hold all the answers about the past," she said. "About what we are a part of."

The sisters looked at each other, and then two pairs of big blue eyes stared up at the queen.

"Will you sing it for us, please?" Elsa asked.

Iduna looked toward the door, debating whether she should humor her daughters. After deciding there was no harm in letting the girls hear the song, she nodded to them. "Okay. Cuddle close. Scooch in," she said, pulling Elsa and Anna to her, tucking them all back under her scarf.

Queen Iduna's voice was low and warm as it sang the lullaby her mother had sung to her. It was the sound of love in the girls' ears, and Anna was fast asleep even before the song was done. The queen picked Anna up gently, cradling her as she carried her across the room. She placed Anna softly on her own bed and pulled up the covers, tucking her in tight. Queen Iduna returned to Elsa just as she finished the song.

"Now sleep, my little snow," she said, kissing both of Elsa's hands.

The queen fluffed Elsa's pillows, stroked her daughter's long hair, and picked up the candle that flickered on the bedside table.

"Mother?" Elsa said as the queen touched the door

of the room. "Do you think Ahtohallan knows why I have magical power?"

Her mother didn't answer immediately. She thought carefully before she spoke. "If Ahtohallan is out there," she said finally, "I imagine it knows that and much more."

Elsa leaned heavily into her pillow. "Someone should really try to find it."

Queen Iduna's smile was bittersweet as she stepped into the hallway and closed the door behind her.

With the echo of her mother's lullaby in her ears, Elsa drifted off to sleep. She dreamed about finding Ahtohallan, and learning the answer to every question she'd ever had . . . and the answers to some of her sister's questions, too.

All of Arendelle was silent, and the night was still— even in the castle—until Anna tiptoed across the rugs of her bedroom floor. It took the five-year-old more than one try to pull herself onto her sister's bed. But once she had made it, she crawled over and shook Elsa's shoulder.

"Elsa," Anna said in what she thought was a whisper but what was really the furthest thing from one. "*Psst*, Elsa. Wake up, wake up, wake up!"

Elsa hated to be awakened. It made her grumpy. "Anna," she protested, turning her back on her sister and tugging her covers up under her chin, "go back to sleep."

"I just can't," Anna complained, flopping on the bed like a young child who hadn't gotten her way . . . and who refused to give up. "The sky's awake. So *I'm* awake. So we have to play."

Anna looked out the window at the dancing greens and blues of the Northern Lights that dominated the night sky. Then she looked back at her sister, who had buried herself under the covers. She poked Elsa. She prodded her. She even tried to pull her blankets off.

"If I agree to play with you for a little bit, will you let me sleep as long as I want when we are done?" asked Elsa's muffled voice from beneath the blankets.

"Yes!" Anna agreed enthusiastically, nodding.

Even with Anna tugging at her, Elsa was a reluctant partner. She rubbed her eyes and dragged her feet as her sister pulled her to the Great Hall—and then her ice magic came out and a new chapter began for them.

CHAPTER 2

One day years later, when the girls were grown, their parents were gone, and Elsa was Queen of Arendelle, the sun was shining brilliantly over the cliffs of the fjord. Elsa stood on a rear castle balcony, waiting for her moment to rejoin the visiting dignitaries and wish them well on their journeys home. She had already spoken to them about trade and commerce, as well as the Arendellian people and their goals for the kingdom. Anna liked to tell her that she was graceful and wise far beyond her years. For people who didn't know Elsa, it was strange at first, but the more she spoke, the more they would have agreed with Anna.

"Your Majesty, they're ready."

Elsa jumped, startled when she heard Kai, one of

her most trusted advisers. Kai had known her since the day she was born. He could tell that Elsa was nervous, but he kept this observation quietly to himself. Her hands were wrapped around the balcony railing, and her emotional jolt instantly turned it to ice. She laughed nervously.

"Oh, ha! Excuse me. I'm coming," she said.

After unfreezing the railing, Elsa turned to follow Kai into the castle, but she was stopped by a haunting call, a voice that spoke to her in a wordless melody. It was beautiful, yet sounded pained at the same time. She turned back toward the outdoors.

"Do you hear that?" she asked Kai, wondering where the voice was coming from.

"What?" Kai answered.

"That voice," Elsa said.

Kai's brow furrowed. "What voice?"

As soon as he said those words, the voice stopped as abruptly as it had started. Elsa turned back to Kai and saw concern on his face. She smiled to cover the unsettling feeling that washed over her.

"Never mind," she said, and followed him into the castle.

Inside, Kristoff was performing daring tricks with Sven. He had already shared with the dignitaries some unusual facts about reindeer that could help them cultivate better crops and make traveling throughout Arendelle easier. As Kristoff finished, Elsa approached the front of the room for her final goodbyes.

Everything's great, Elsa thought, regaining her composure with a smile. Her muscles were tense with the urge to release her magic.

"Thank you again for coming," Elsa said to each dignitary as they passed. "It's always great to see you." Once she had completed her duty, Elsa exited the room and walked along the hallways and out the castle's front door. She greeted the villagers and visitors scattered throughout the courtyard as she strolled toward the fjord.

Elsa passed small boats and magnificent ships tied to the docks. She stayed calm as she went as far down the side of the fjord as she could, until there were no people or boats around. This was where she went when she had to release extra energy. Whoever or whatever the voice was that had spoken to her in its wordless melody had filled her with more energy and magic than she'd ever felt before.

Elsa threw out her arms and let magic shoot from her fingers at full force. Ice and snow filled the air in front of her, then crashed into the fjord. Elsa turned and covered her face, chuckling as water splashed all around her.

CHAPTER 3

Anna walked along the edge of the village and took a deep breath of the fresh autumn air as a bright red leaf blew past her. It was the perfect day to find the perfect pumpkin. She saw one of her favorite friends up ahead, and she couldn't help the huge smile that took over her face.

"Enjoying your new permafrost, Olaf?" she asked the talking snowman, who was sunbathing happily amid the pumpkins in the patch with a satisfied grin on his face.

"I'm just living the dream, Anna," he said, reaching out to catch the same brilliant red leaf as it flew by him. "Oh, how I wish this could last forever."

Anna closed her eyes as she took a moment to let the warm sunshine wash over her body. "Mmmm." Suddenly remembering why she had come to the patch in the first place, Anna opened her eyes and set out searching for the perfect pumpkin. It had to have no holes or cuts. She also wanted one with a nice thick green stem. And maybe one that wasn't lopsided. Anna bent to knock on one with her knuckles. It sounded hollow. She didn't remember whether that meant the pumpkin was good or bad, but she supposed it really didn't matter, since they weren't planning to eat it. Still, she kept looking.

"And yet change mocks us with her beauty," Olaf said.

"What's that?" Anna asked, carefully inspecting each pumpkin she passed. One had a bug hole. And the one next to that wasn't quite the right orange for a perfect pumpkin.

"Forgive me. Maturity is making me poetic," he mused. "Tell me—you're older and thus all-knowing. Do you ever worry about the notion that nothing is permanent?"

"Nope," she answered right away, but she was only half listening. The perfect pumpkin was proving to be rather hard to find.

"Really," he said, bewildered by her response. "Wow, I can't wait until I'm aged like you, so I don't have to worry about important things."

Taking a break from her pumpkin hunt, Anna concentrated on Olaf's question. "That's not what I mean," she explained. "I don't worry, because . . . well, I have you and Elsa and Kristoff and Sven, and the gates are open wide, and I'm not alone anymore—" She lay down next to him, her head cradled in her arms, and looked up at the bright blue sky, wondering how to explain her thoughts to her friend. She had an idea and sat up, motioning to a rotting pumpkin in the patch. She explained that one day it would become fertilizer to help other pumpkins grow. But Olaf still wasn't sure what she was saying.

Taking his hand, Anna pulled him to his feet. They left the pumpkin patch—and right next to the gate was the perfect pumpkin. Anna grabbed it and held it as she and Olaf walked along the road into town. She tried to explain that while some things in the world changed, other things didn't—those things could be counted on to always stay the same. Anna hoisted her perfect pumpkin onto a cart led by a gray horse driven by a gray-haired villager. She waved at the driver as he headed toward town.

A big family, full of grandparents, parents, babies,

and other children, called a greeting to Anna and Olaf. Olaf wanted to point out to Anna that the people in the family had changed—some had grown old, and new members had been born. But before he began to speak, Anna pulled him over to a house that was being painted.

"Don't you love this color?" she said. Anna asked the painter the name of it while Olaf tried to say that the house had been white and was now being painted blue, so that was changing as well.

Anna didn't hear him. "See, Olaf?" she said with a smile, taking his hand in hers. "Some things never change."

CHAPTER 4

The red leaf finally blew out of Olaf's hand and traveled on until it passed Kristoff and his reindeer, Sven. Kristoff was showing Sven a ring box.

"Are you sure you're ready to ask her the big question?" Kristoff asked in Sven's voice.

"Yes," Kristoff replied to Sven, as if the reindeer had said the words himself. "I'm just not sure how to ask her in the most romantic way without messing everything up."

"Let me handle the details!" Sven's voice said.

Kristoff knew Anna was the one he was supposed to spend the rest of his life with, so he was confident he'd find the right words when the time was right. He swooned when he saw Anna walking down the street toward them with Olaf by her side, window shopping. Kristoff held tightly to Sven to ease his nerves as he looked at her. Maybe he wasn't as confident as he thought.

Kristoff pulled his best friend into a suit shop. He needed to find the last perfect touch for his outfit. He looked through neckties and ascots. He saw ones with stripes and ones with dots, but they weren't what he was looking for. Then Sven found an ascot covered in carrots and nudged it toward him.

"It's perfect!" Kristoff declared.

The red leaf flew farther through the air until it reached the castle, where a huge gust swept it through an open window into the library. The papers Elsa was working on flew off her desk and fluttered around the room.

She stood and walked through the dancing papers to the window and looked down at the kingdom, wondering if the changing winds were signaling a big change to come. Maybe that was why she'd heard the haunting call.

When her eyes landed on Anna and Kristoff hugging after his trip to the suit shop, a smile immediately lit up her face. Sven and Olaf weren't far behind, laughing, snorting, and doing the things that reindeer and snowmen did when they were having fun.

More than anything, Elsa wanted moments like this to stay the same. They were so precious to her, she wished she could freeze them. She realized the best thing she could do was join her sister and friends to seize the day and be part of the moment. Without another thought for her paperwork, Elsa rushed out the door.

CHAPTER 5

Olaf, Kristoff, Anna, and Sven were in the center of the village when Elsa caught up with them. The people of Arendelle cheered for their queen, dancing and singing around her, celebrating the bounty that the season had brought to Arendelle. Anna danced with them and helped the villagers with the harvest they had set on the main table under the autumn sky. As usual, she made sure everything was just right for everyone.

Olaf even helped unload the fishing boats. The first person at the boat grabbed a fish and tossed it to the next person in line, and the fish was passed all the way down to the cooking area. The system worked great—except Olaf was at the end of the line, and instead of passing each fish to the cook, he innocently tossed them back into the sea.

Elsa found herself next to Anna as she proudly raised the Arendellian flag. When the flag reached the top of the pole, it snapped in the wind, waving a welcome to all who saw it.

Anna took Elsa's arm and they stood together next to the flagpole. They were proud to live in a kingdom of plenty, under a flag that stood for the good of everyone. They promised their people, and themselves, that the flag would always fly.

The villagers laughed and chatted as they made their way to their places at the communal tables. They had more than they could have ever wanted, and they hoped for their good luck to last. The pumpkin Anna had picked sat on the head table, a perfect decoration for an amazing celebration. Elsa stood behind her chair with the castle shining radiantly behind her. As queen, she was the first to take her seat. She quickly signaled for everyone else to follow.

Anna stood a moment longer, her warm gaze passing over the people and the kingdom she loved. Friends and family passed food to one another as they talked excitedly. Everyone was grateful for the time they had together.

As the sun set and the crowd dispersed, everyone

with a full belly, Anna held the castle door open for her family—Elsa, Sven, Kristoff, and Olaf—as they stepped inside, one by one. Then she closed the door, excited for what they had planned next.

CHAPTER 6

In the castle library that night, the fire blazed in the hearth, the red and orange flames dancing brightly. It was a warm and safe place to gather and have fun with family and friends—the opposite of the cold day during the eternal winter when Hans had put the fire out and left Anna there all alone.

Elsa, Olaf, and Kristoff huddled together on a small couch. They were all trying to guess what Anna was acting out in a game of charades. Sven was keeping score. He was also in charge of ringing the bell when the time was up.

Elsa stared at her sister in confusion. She had no idea who or what Anna was trying to depict. It could have been a lizard, or it could have been a ship. She sat back, utterly stumped as she watched Anna make silly, monsterlike faces.

"Okay," Kristoff said, sure that he had the right answer. "Lion."

"Grizzly bear," Olaf said.

"Monster," Kristoff guessed.

"Brown bear," said Olaf.

"Angry face!" Kristoff yelled.

"Black bear," Olaf said, continuing his string of bear guesses.

Anna knew she had to do something different or her family would never guess the right answer. An idea suddenly came to her. She pretended to grab a sword and attacked the air in front of her as if it were an invisible enemy.

"Hans!" Olaf shouted immediately.

They remembered the prince from the Southern Isles who had betrayed Anna—and all of Arendelle—three years before. Anna motioned to let Olaf know he almost had it.

"Unredeemable monster," Elsa said, referring to Hans, finally able to jump in.

"Greatest mistake of your life!" Kristoff yelled.

"Wouldn't even kiss you!" Olaf added.

Sven rang the bell, held delicately between his teeth, to let them know they'd run out of time. Anna was surprised they hadn't guessed correctly, but she liked how their answers had so accurately described Hans. They looked at her expectantly. "Villain," she said.

Groans filled the room. Hans was definitely a villain.

"We all *kind of* got it," Olaf said.

Everyone nodded as Anna took a seat on the couch next to Elsa.

"Okay, Olaf," Kristoff prompted. "You're up."

"Okay," the snowman said. "So much easier now that I can read!" He reached into the hat that Sven held to pick out a piece of paper and read what was on it. "Lightning round, boys against girls."

Kristoff was fired up. "I'm ready, I'm ready. Go!"

Sven turned to reset the timer and then rang the bell.

Olaf had an advantage in playing charades because he could rearrange himself to fit any answer, and that was exactly what he did now. He pulled out his arms and legs and nose and put them in different places on his body to form different shapes and sizes. Almost as fast as Olaf assembled himself each time, Kristoff guessed the right answer.

"Unicorn," Kristoff said. "Ice cream. Castle! Oaken! Teapot! Mouse! Oooh, Elsa!"

Sven rang the bell to end the round. Time had flown! The guys cheered. They hadn't gotten a single one wrong.

Anna didn't believe it was fair. "I don't think Olaf should get to rearrange," she said, looking pointedly at both Olaf and Kristoff. Elsa's expression showed that she agreed. "Doesn't matter. This is going to be a cinch. Two sisters, one mind."

Elsa didn't have her sister's confidence as she got to her feet to choose the paper from Sven. "Thank you," she said.

"Okay," Anna said with conviction. "Here we go! You got this, Elsa." She had no doubt they could still win.

Then Sven rang the bell and Elsa started acting out her first charade. Anna immediately realized that picking charades for family game night had been a huge mistake. While Elsa was great with magic, she was horrible at charades. Nothing Elsa did made any sense. Every motion she made just seemed so . . . vague.

"Any time. Just do it with your body," Anna said, coaching her. Then she simply started guessing. "Um . . . nothing. Air. Tree. People. Treeple! That's not a word. Shovel boy. Teeth? Oh, pillow fort!"

"Polar bear!" Olaf shouted, not wanting to be left out.

"Hey!" Anna said. He wasn't allowed to guess. And he already had a billion points with Kristoff. Besides, it was boys versus girls.

"Sorry," he said.

Elsa looked at the paper again, and as she tried to imagine how to act out the word, she heard the beautifully haunting voice again. Her heart raced and her palms sweated. She looked at her friends, but they were oblivious, still trying to guess what she was acting out. Elsa spun around, searching for the source of the voice.

"Mountains," Anna said. "Teeth. Did I already say teeth? Ooh. Uh. Distracted. Um, worried? Panicking? Disturbed."

Elsa didn't even hear her sister. All she heard was the voice.

"Oh, come on—you definitely look disturbed," Anna said.

The bell rang again, signaling that time was up. Anna groaned.

"We won," Kristoff announced to the room.

Anna wasn't ready to give in. She jumped off the couch, ready to go again.

"Rematch?" she asked, already mentally adding a new rule. She would make sure the group agreed that Olaf couldn't rearrange his body this time.

But even though it had stopped as suddenly as it had started, Elsa couldn't help thinking about the haunting call. She knew she wouldn't be able to concentrate on the game.

"Oh, you know what?" she said. "I think I'll turn in." *Where is the voice coming from? Why am I the only one who can hear it?*

Anna could see that something wasn't right. Elsa never went to bed early unless there was a major event in the morning. And she never left early from family game night.

"Are you okay?" she asked.

Elsa paused in the doorway and nodded. "Just tired. Good night." She smiled and moved down the hallway.

CHAPTER 7

Still surprised at Elsa's leaving, Anna stared after her sister.

"Yeah," Olaf said. "I'm tired, too. And Sven promised to read me a bedtime story—didn't you, Sven?"

Kristoff's heart pounded. He couldn't leave yet—that wasn't part of his plan.

"Did I?" he asked, speaking in Sven's voice.

Olaf smiled at Sven. "Oh, you do the best voices." He jumped up off the couch and headed for the door. "Like when you pretend to be Kristoff. And you're like, 'I just need to go talk to some rocks about my childhood and stuff.'"

Kristoff waved them away. He needed to be alone with Anna.

"How about you guys start without me?" he said.

Olaf and Sven looked at each other, nodded in agreement, then left.

Anna immediately started cleaning up the mess from their game. She returned the bell to the cabinet drawer and set the timer back on its shelf. While her back was turned, Kristoff raced around the room to set his idea in motion. He threw fresh logs on the fire, then wound up a music box to set a relaxed mood. He quickly chewed on a mint leaf to freshen his breath while he straightened his shirt and tugged at his collar, making sure his ascot adorned with carrots was perfectly in place. Then he did exactly what he had planned to do.

Kristoff pulled the ring out of his pocket and stood behind Anna. It seemed like the right time to ask her the one question he'd been waiting to ask. Just as he opened his mouth . . .

"Did Elsa seem weird to you?" Anna asked, her back still to him.

Kristoff wasn't sure what she meant. "She seemed like Elsa?" he responded. Then he took a deep breath and got down on one knee.

"That last word really seemed to throw her." Anna bent down to look through the discarded paper clues on the floor. "What was it?"

"I don't know," Kristoff said in a scratchy voice that didn't sound familiar. He cleared his throat. "Ahem . . ." Then, in a deep voice: "I don't know. But, um—"

Anna read all the game clues, but none of them seemed to be Elsa's. Then she saw another, off to the side by the table. She reached for it. "Ice?" she said in disbelief. "Oh, come on!" Anna threw her arms out in frustration, making Kristoff jump back in surprise. The ring flew out of his hand and slid under the couch. He dove to get it back.

"She couldn't act out *ice*?" Anna asked, confused. Even if her sister was the worst charades player in the world, the one word she should have been able to depict was *ice*. "I better go check on her." She stood and kissed Kristoff just as he got back on one knee. "Thanks, honey. Love you!" And then she was gone without having seen what he had in his hand.

Kristoff held the ring and looked after her. He sighed in disappointment. "Love you, too. It's fine." The music box slowly wound down, echoing the deflated mood in the room.

CHAPTER 8

Elsa stood at her bedroom window, deep in thought, while the Northern Lights shone blue and green around her. She recognized Anna's special knock on her door, the one her sister had been doing ever since they were children, and smiled.

"Come in," she said.

Anna noticed something familiar as soon as she walked into the room. Elsa had their mother's beautiful burgundy scarf draped around her shoulders. It brought back memories of how their mother had always wrapped them in it, held them close, keeping them secure and protected. Anna remembered the feelings of comfort and of love.

"Yep. Something's wrong," she said.

Elsa continued to stare out the window as if she were waiting for someone, or something, before she finally turned to look at her sister. "With you?"

"No, with you," Anna said. "You're wearing Mother's scarf. You do that when something's wrong." It suddenly hit her and she gasped, realizing what the problem could be. "Did we hurt your feelings? I'm so sorry if we did. You know, very few people are actually good at family games. That's just a fact."

"No . . . that's not it," Elsa insisted. She paused, debating whether she should tell her sister about the voice she'd been hearing.

"Then what is it?" Anna asked.

Elsa hesitated a moment longer, then said, "There's this . . . I just don't want to mess things up."

Anna grabbed Elsa's hands and led her to the bed to sit down. "What things?" she asked, her eyes full of concern. "You're doing great! Oh, Elsa—when are you going to see yourself the way I see you?"

Elsa knew her sister was right, and that made her feel good. She pressed her forehead against Anna's. "What would I do without you?"

Anna knew the answer without thinking about it. "You'll always have me." Elsa smiled back at her. Anna climbed onto the bed and leaned back against the pillows. "I know what you need. Come on, come here."

"What?" Elsa asked.

"In Mama's words: *'Cuddle close . . . scooch in,'*" Anna said.

Elsa moved next to her sister and let Anna wrap the scarf tightly around her shoulders. Anna sang the lullaby from their childhood to her, the one that never failed to remind them of their mother. It had always soothed her sister, and she hoped it still did. She rubbed Elsa's forehead with her finger, like their mother had when they were young.

"I know what you're doing," Elsa said, even as her eyes blinked sleepily and then closed completely. It wasn't long before she fell asleep.

Anna smiled; their mother had always known best. She yawned and stretched her arms up. It was late, and she was tired, too. Without another thought, she lay down and fell asleep next to her sister.

CHAPTER 9

*L*ater that night, dreams filled Elsa's head. She was walking through a forest filled with beautiful trees, covered in golden sunshine. She heard a laugh and saw a young boy and girl playing in a pile of leaves. But the leaves they threw hovered high in the air, impossibly high, and they stayed there, not falling. A reindeer ran by. Whether it was running to something or from something, Elsa couldn't tell.

If Anna had been awake, she would have seen that the images from Elsa's dream were suspended in the air above her sister, made from soft flakes of snow. It was like a memory, playing for Elsa and anyone else in the room. But Elsa's dreams had never physically manifested themselves in snow before.

Elsa suddenly woke and sat up, and her dreams dissolved into a snowfall that drifted down and covered the bed. *Where did this come from?* she thought. She looked around in the darkness and listened. At first, she didn't see or hear anything. Then the voice began calling to her in its quiet melody.

She glanced at Anna, but her sister was sound asleep. As quietly as she could, Elsa slipped from the bed and moved quickly to the window, hoping to find something outside that would tell her where the sound was coming from. She saw nothing out of the ordinary.

Elsa backed away from the window and out of the room. The sound had never lasted this long before—it had appeared and disappeared just as quickly. Now it followed her as she raced along the hall.

Even while looking for its source, she tried to ignore the call and wish it away. Everyone she had ever loved was here in Arendelle. She'd already had the biggest adventure of her life and didn't want to risk following a voice into something unknown that might take them away from her. She almost managed to convince herself it was just a ringing in her ears.

As Elsa opened the castle's back door and stepped outside, a thought occurred to her. *Maybe the call is coming from someone with magic.* Though she would never admit it, deep down she felt she wasn't meant to be queen. Every day, as she felt her power grow stronger, it became a little harder for her to deny her doubts and fears, which grew stronger every day. Maybe the mysterious voice knew that and wanted to help her. Elsa decided to answer it, echoing its call.

She heard the voice and responded. Every time it reached for her in song, she answered.

As she walked farther away from the castle, along the outskirts of the village and toward the waters of the fjord, Elsa tentatively used her magic as an answer to the voice. Power surged from her hands, and she threw snow up into the air. The snow formed a forest that was just like the one from her dream— a dream she no longer remembered.

Elsa walked through the fantastical snowy landscape, creating amazing imagery—a swirling wind full of leaves, a salamander, a water horse, and rock giants. She chased the creatures, fascinated by what her magic had made. And the beautifully haunting call led her every step of the way.

The voice led her farther north. Elsa used her power to build a hill of ice that jutted into the sky over the fjord. As she climbed to the top, the voice began to fade. Elsa realized she didn't want it to leave her. She wanted to follow the call into the unknown. She let her arms fall to her sides and looked at the sky, surrendering herself and her power to the voice. Just then, a wave of magic shot out from her, freezing all the moisture in the air into small crystal symbols that spread across the land.

Elsa looked at them in awe. Each of the crystals had one of four symbols on them, and she recognized them.

"Air, fire, water, earth . . . ," she said aloud.

CHAPTER 10

Something had awakened Anna, and she wasn't sure what. Looking at the bed next to her, she saw that Elsa was gone. In her place were soft flakes of freshly fallen snow.

"Elsa?" she called. All she heard was silence.

The light coming in the window seemed different. Curious, Anna stepped out onto the balcony, her mother's scarf wrapped tightly around her shoulders. The air was full of frozen crystals as far as she could see. The crystals refracted the colors from the Northern Lights, sending them all around. She looked in amazement—and then spotted Elsa far away, near the fjord.

Just then, a mighty blast of light appeared from the north.

The crystals began to fall in a cascade, starting from farthest away, crashing to the ground without mercy. The villagers of Arendelle came to their windows and doors, holding each other close as the ice shattered on the cobblestones in front of their homes. And then, one by one, the lanterns around the village went out, leaving the only light to come from the moon.

Anna knew she had to help the villagers. Eyes wide, she ran through the darkened castle, stumbling her way around before bursting out the doors right on the heels of Kristoff and Olaf. She didn't notice the lack of light—she just knew she had to find her sister. Running toward the fjord, Anna saw the water fountains drying up. She tried to make sense of it. The villagers tried, too, opening their doors to look for answers as she passed by.

The wind whipped up and banged open shutters and windows. It was so strong, people were pushed from their homes and onto the streets. Anna, Kristoff, and Olaf did what they could to help, but they, too, were being blown across the streets and toward the bridge.

In the stables, Sven watched all the water disappear from his trough and those of the other animals. He looked up and gave a confused grunt when a gust of wind blew the double doors in and they slammed against the wall. Then he pushed his stall door open with his antlers and headed out to the village. It was time to find Kristoff and the others.

Elsa, who had raced back to the castle once the ice crystals had started falling, stopped suddenly. "The air rages, no fire, no water . . . the earth is next. We have to get out." And just like that, the cobblestones began to ripple like wheat in a breeze and shuttled people down the village streets.

"We're being pushed out!" a villager shouted. His body was forced up a path that led to the cliffs.

Elsa ran deeper into the village to help the people of Arendelle get to safety.

"It'll be okay!" she shouted. "Evacuate to the cliffs!"

"Oh, no!" Olaf yelled as he tried to hold on to a pole on the bridge. "I'm gonna blow!"

Kristoff grabbed Olaf and as many children as he could just as Sven walked up. Kristoff had never been more grateful to see his best friend. He placed his load on the reindeer's back.

"I've got you. Wow, you're heavy," he said to Olaf. He nodded to the cliffs, where the others were gathering.

Sven grunted and headed off. The parents of the children who rode on him followed right behind, refusing to lose track of them.

Anna joined Elsa and the others, helping to make sure everyone got out of the village safely. She couldn't leave anyone behind in these dangerous conditions. Kristoff called to the sisters to lead their people, because the Arendellians needed them. He stayed in the rear, aiding those who couldn't keep up.

Working together, Anna and Elsa finally got everyone to the top of the cliffs over the fjord. When Anna looked back for Kristoff, she was happy to see that he was near. Behind him, the Arendelle flag that always flew at the center of the village was ripped off its pole by the violent wind. And as Anna gasped in surprise, the wind suddenly died. Everything went silent.

CHAPTER 11

The villagers formed small groups, whispering, shaking their heads, and patting backs as they comforted each other. Children huddled close to their parents as everyone tried to make sense of what had just happened.

One half-asleep villager looked around in confusion, wondering why he was no longer in his bed but was instead standing on top of a cliff. He blinked sleepily as Olaf and some of the Arendellian children twirled by, spun by the wind and covered in the ice crystals that had just fallen from the sky. The villager shook his head, thinking he was quite possibly having the weirdest dream he'd ever had.

The sound of Sven's hoofs on the stones of the

cliff's path announced his and Kristoff's arrival. The reindeer's back was piled high with blankets, which Kristoff passed out as the two comforted the villagers.

"Yes, everyone's out and safe," he assured an older woman as he pressed a warm woolen shawl in her hands. "Take one of these."

As the duo made their way around the groups, they passed Olaf, who sat on the ground surrounded by children. The kids laughed as they found Elsa's fallen ice crystals and pressed them into Olaf's snow body. Kristoff and Sven shared a puzzled glance when they saw his bizarre decorations.

"You okay, there, Olaf?" Kristoff asked.

The snowman nodded. "We're calling this controlling what you can when things feel out of control."

Kristoff nodded. It seemed logical.

Raised voices made him turn his head. He saw Anna and Elsa standing close together, and neither looked happy. He was torn between joining the sisters and giving them space.

"Okay, I don't understand—you have been hearing a voice and didn't think to tell me?" asked Anna.

Elsa cheeks colored. She felt ashamed for keeping her secret. "I didn't want to worry you," she said.

"We made a promise not to shut each other out," Anna reminded her. "Just tell me—what's going on?"

Elsa sighed, and then blurted out, "I woke the magical spirts of the Enchanted Forest."

At a loss for words, Anna could only stare at her sister as Kristoff and Sven slowly approached. "Okay, that's definitely not what I thought you were going to say," Anna said, searching her memories. "The Enchanted Forest? The one Father warned us about?"

"Yes," Elsa said, nodding.

"Why would you do that?" Anna asked. Nothing about the night was making sense.

"Because of the voice," Elsa said. "I know it sounds crazy, but I believe whoever is calling me is good."

Anna glanced sharply at her sister. "How can you say that?" she demanded, throwing an arm out toward the dark and empty village. "Look at our kingdom."

Elsa sighed. She understood what Anna was saying, but deep inside she somehow knew the voice meant them no harm. "It's just that my magic can feel it. *I can feel it.*"

Anna stared at her sister. Her emotions wavered as many questions ran through her head. But they all led to the same conclusion: her sister would do the right thing.

"Okay," she said.

Elsa smiled, grateful once again that Anna believed in her.

CHAPTER 12

Rocks began to dance on the ground just then, and the villagers panicked. It was the second time in one night that their world had been shaken.

"Oh, no," said Anna. "What now?"

But Kristoff knew that this movement was far different from what had happened before.

"Trolls?" he asked in surprise. He rushed to the mountain pass just as a bunch of familiar-looking boulders tumbled through. The boulders rolled toward Elsa and Anna and popped open to reveal mountain trolls. They were thrilled to see Kristoff and Sven and jumped onto the two of them, knocking Kristoff over in their excitement.

"Kristoff!" said Bulda, the troll who had raised Kristoff since he was very young. "We missed you!"

"Grand Pabbie!" Elsa said, recognizing the wise leader of the mountain trolls as he rolled right up to her.

"Well, never a dull moment with you two. I hope you are prepared for what you have done, Elsa. Angry magical spirits are not for the faint of heart," the elder troll said.

"Why are they still angry?" she asked. They couldn't possibly still be mad over what had happened when Anna and Elsa's father was a child—or could they? "What does this have to do with Arendelle?"

"Hmm," Grand Pabbie mused. "Let me see what I can see."

Grand Pabbie turned his gaze up to the sky. He waved his hands, stirring the Northern Lights into motion. "The past is not what it seems. A wrong demands to be righted; the truth must be found. Without it . . . I see no future."

The words worried Anna. "No future?"

Grand Pabbie lowered his hands and let the sky return to its normal patterns. He focused on Elsa, concern in his eyes. "When one can see no future, all one can do is the next right thing."

"The next right thing is for me to go to the Enchanted Forest and find that voice," said Elsa with resolve. "Kristoff, can I borrow your wagon . . . and Sven?" Elsa asked.

Kristoff raised an eyebrow. "I'm not very comfortable with the idea of that."

Anna refused to let Elsa go by herself. "You are not going alone," she insisted.

Elsa shook her head. "Anna, I have my powers to protect me. You don't."

"Wait, what, excuse me, pardon?" Anna asked, putting her hands on her hips and staring directly at her sister. "If I recall, your powers have mostly just gotten you into trouble. Protecting you has been my job."

Grand Pabbie nodded in agreement. "She does have a point."

Anna smiled at the troll. "Thank you." Then she turned to her sister. "I'm coming."

Kristoff chose that moment to enter the conversation.

"Me too," he added, not wanting to be left out of an adventure. "I'll drive."

"I'll bring the snacks!" Olaf said as the wind twirled him past them, the crystals that clung to him sparkling in the moonlight.

Elsa was reluctant to accept, but as she looked between Anna and Kristoff, she knew her only choice was to agree. She nodded before turning to Grand Pabbie.

"Will you look after our people?" Elsa asked. She was eager to leave and make the kingdom safe again, but was concerned for what the villagers would do until that happened.

"Of course," Grand Pabbie said.

"Please make sure they stay out of the kingdom until we return," Anna added.

"Thank you," Elsa said, trusting the wise troll with the lives of her people the way her parents had trusted him with the life of her sister. "Let's let them know," she said to Kristoff, and the two of them rushed to tell everyone the news.

Grand Pabbie motioned for Anna to move close to him. "Anna, I am worried for her. We have always feared Elsa's powers were too much for this world. Now we must pray they are enough."

Anna nodded, unable to conceal the worry on her own face. "I won't let anything happen to her."

CHAPTER 13

Early the next morning, as the sunrise painted the fjords of Arendelle in warm colors, Elsa, Anna, Olaf, Kristoff, and Sven set out on their journey.

"Hyah!" Kristoff called, holding Sven's reins. The reindeer trotted forward, pulling the wagon with the rest of the group in it.

Olaf broke the silence, not realizing that everyone was lost in their own thoughts of what might happen during their travels.

"Who's into trivia?" he asked gleefully. No one answered, so he responded to himself. "I am! Okay!"

Anna caught Elsa's eye across the snowman's head. They smiled at each other and settled in for the trip, listening to Olaf spout off his fun facts.

He had always been interested in unusual tidbits of information, but ever since he'd learned to read, his interest had grown tremendously.

"Did you know that water has memory?" he asked.

His friends found some of his facts to be interesting, but some were just plain strange.

"Did you know . . . gorillas burp when they are happy?" Olaf chirped.

As the miles and hours went by, they passed the sparkling waterfalls in the mountains around the fjord as the sun beat down on them from its highest point of the day. Olaf continued with his never-ending list of facts. This time when Elsa caught Anna's glance, they both slowly shook their heads and rolled their eyes.

When the sun began to set, they finally reached the magnificent ice palace Elsa had built for herself. The sisters stared at it, remembering Elsa's coronation day three years before.

When Anna had approached her sister and asked for her blessing to marry Hans, she and Elsa had fought. Elsa had found it ridiculous that Anna wanted to marry a man she had just met. And because of that, Elsa's magical secret, which she had worked so hard to keep hidden, was revealed during their spat, when Anna accidentally pulled off one of Elsa's gloves and ice shot from her hand.

Anna had felt so lost when Elsa ran off. But she didn't blame Elsa. If she had been accused of sorcery by the Duke of Weselton, Anna probably would have run away, too. But Anna didn't care if her sister could freeze things, or even if she could set things on fire. She had just wanted to be with her and for the two of them to be sisters again. Instead, all she could feel was the hurt that had consumed her after calling out to Elsa as her sister ran farther and farther away. Anna couldn't imagine how lonely and afraid Elsa had been, too.

As Elsa stared at her beautiful ice palace, her thoughts also returned to that day. She remembered how scared she'd been—scared she would hurt Anna and others with her power if she stayed, and scared that her people would think she was a monster once they saw what her powers could do. She had held back tears as Anna called her name. She knew her sister had wanted her to come back. But all Elsa could think about in that moment was running as far away from Arendelle as possible so she could protect Anna, like she'd always tried to do.

Elsa's confidence had grown when she realized the full extent of what she could do with her magic. It wasn't until after Anna had sacrificed herself for Elsa, because of the true love she felt for her sister, that Elsa finally embraced the truth. Her magic wasn't a curse.

It wasn't meant to hurt people. Elsa could do more than build snowmen and make beautiful icy patterns. She had constructed a magnificent ice palace that still stood strong today. Her magic was, and always had been, a gift.

Olaf's giggle pulled Elsa out of her memories.

"Did you know men are six times more likely to be struck by lightning?" the snowman told whoever was still listening. "Sorry, Kristoff."

They kept going, over the ridge beyond the ice palace, farther north than they had ever gone before.

CHAPTER 14

"**D**id you know we blink four million times a day?" Olaf blurted out. "Did you know wombats poop squares? Did you know donkeys sink but mules don't?"

Kristoff didn't mind that Olaf was full of facts, but his head was about to explode from all the talking. So he jumped in when Olaf took a breath. "Did you know sleeping quietly on long journeys prevents insanity?"

Olaf thought about it. "That doesn't sound true."

Elsa, Anna, and Sven immediately agreed with Kristoff, nodding vigorously.

"It's true," said Anna.

"It's absolutely true," said Elsa.

"Gruunnt," said Sven.

The snowman shrugged. "Well, that was unanimous,

but I will look it up when I get home." He lay back in the hay and watched as Elsa created an ice blanket for him. She placed it over him, making sure he was completely covered. Then she kissed him on his forehead.

"Good night," she said.

After tucking the blanket under his chin, Olaf finally went to sleep.

Elsa began to yawn when she saw Olaf snuggled in so cozily. It had been a long night for everyone. She pulled her mother's scarf out of Anna's bag and wrapped it around her shoulders. Then she nestled down in the hay and drifted to sleep next to her friend.

Anna took the opportunity to climb from the back of the wagon up to the front bench and sit with Kristoff. "They're both asleep," she reported. She straightened her clothes, pulled hay from her hair, and checked to make sure her breath smelled fresh. "So, what do you want to do?" She snuggled up against him.

Kristoff grinned. "I can think of something," he said, tossing the reins to Sven before digging in his pocket. "Sven, keep us steady, will yah?

Sven's gait changed to a romantic little prance as he grunted his support.

Anna smiled, closing her eyes as she pursed her lips together and leaned in to Kristoff for a kiss.

But Kristoff was so nervous, he missed her cue. "Anna. Ahem." He cleared his throat and tried again. "Anna, remember our first trip like this, when I said you'd have to be crazy to want to marry a man you just met?"

Anna's eyes widened and she scooted far enough down the front bench that Marshmallow could have sat between them. "Wait, what?" she asked. "Crazy? You didn't say I was crazy. You think I'm crazy?"

"No, I did. You were . . ." He tried to explain, but stopped short at Sven's warning grunt. Kristoff wanted to save the moment, to bring it back on course. He couldn't mess this up again. "Not crazy, clearly," he said dramatically. "Ha, just *naive.*"

But apparently being naive was even more offensive to Anna. She crossed her arms over her chest, leaned back in the seat, and gave Kristoff a long look. Feeling confused, Kristoff glanced at Sven, who was shaking his head in dismay. Kristoff scrambled for words to dig himself out of the ditch he had tumbled into.

"Not naive. Just new . . . to love. Like I was. And when you're new, you're bound to get it wrong," he finished with confidence. But that confidence quickly deflated.

"So you're saying I'm wrong for you?" Anna asked, one eyebrow raised.

"What?" Kristoff asked in alarm. "No. No, no, no." He took a breath to try to gather his thoughts. "I'm not saying you're not wrong or crazy. I'm saying that it's—"

Anna and Kristoff were so intent on their conversation that neither saw Elsa wake and sit straight up, her expression serious as she looked around, searching for something.

"Kristoff, stop," she said.

He reached for the reins and pulled on them as he asked Sven to bring the wagon to a halt.

"Good idea," he mumbled, knowing he had botched his chance to ask Anna to marry him, again.

"I hear it. I hear the voice," Elsa said firmly.

"You do?" Anna asked, her attention now on her sister. "Olaf, wake up."

Elsa jumped out of the wagon and rushed over to a small rise at the edge of the road. What she saw overwhelmed her with emotion. The others joined her and gasped in awe at what lay before them.

CHAPTER 15

The morning light shone on a magical mist that stood like a wall across a wide, flat plain down below them—a wall that barred them from going any farther. Elsa wondered if it was the impenetrable mist that surrounded the Enchanted Forest. *Have we finally reached it?* she thought. It seemed possible. The mist appeared to enshroud a forest of tall trees—the tops of which they saw poking out of the ceiling of the mist. But everything else in the Enchanted Forest was hidden behind the haze and the rolling particles of colored lights that flashed like lightning bugs as they danced through the mist. Elsa's heart raced, and she couldn't resist the pull she felt any longer. She quickly climbed down the side of the cliff, and the others followed.

Elsa ran across the plain, straight toward the Enchanted Forest. Anna did her best to keep up. Then Elsa stopped before she reached the cloudlike mass and stared at it in silence.

Kristoff was not as patient. He walked past the two girls and approached the mist in wonder. He reached out a hand and pressed it against the gray surface. His hand sprang back like it had hit a bouncy ball.

Olaf watched, fascinated. What had happened to Kristoff's hand gave him an idea. He took a few steps back and charged at the gray cloud as fast as he could. His body bounced off it as if he were hitting a balloon. He giggled as he flew through the air and landed on the ground. All this time, he had thought the journey north would be dangerous. This was fun!

Olaf ran at the mist again. He bounced back again, so he did the only thing he could—he bounced off the mist over and over, laughing hysterically each time.

Anna moved to stand next to Elsa as they stared at the rolling mist. Elsa took a deep breath and grabbed Anna's hand for strength, and the two of them approached.

For them, the mist sparkled and pulled back, revealing four towering stones with a symbol at the top of each one.

"Air, fire, water, earth," Elsa said, naming each one

and knowing they were the same symbols she had seen on the ice crystals in the sky.

With every step they took, the mist parted further to let them through. Sven trailed after them and called out for Kristoff.

Kristoff saw that the curtain of clouds had parted. He caught Olaf's attention, and they walked up behind the sisters with Sven.

"Promise me—we'll do this together," Anna said to Elsa.

"I promise," Elsa agreed.

Kristoff grabbed Anna's hand and put an arm around Sven. Olaf grabbed Elsa's hand. As they all walked farther inside the mist together, it closed behind them and sealed them in.

CHAPTER 16

The mist sparkled. Swirling particles of color danced throughout it. Sven watched, grunting nervously.

"It's okay," Kristoff said to calm his friend.

"Did you know that an enchanted forest is a place of transformation?" Olaf asked, his face full of joy. "I have no idea what that means, but I can't wait to see what it's going to do to each of us."

The flashes of color were mesmerizing, until the lights came together and formed ribbons behind the group. The mist moved forward and touched them. But now when it connected with the friends, they didn't bounce off. Instead, the mist shoved them forward!

The group shouted out in a blur of voices.

"Hey!"

"What the——?"

"No pushing!"

"What *is* this?"

"Too fast!"

"Tree!" Kristoff grunted as he was pushed straight into a trunk. As he untangled himself, the mist pushed him up to join his group.

They stumbled over rocks and tree roots as they ran, getting turned around in confusion before the mist shoved them completely out of its grasp.

"What was that?" Kristoff asked, thoroughly dazed as he stared at the wall of mist that now seemed as calm as when they had viewed it for the very first time.

Olaf was back to bouncing on it like before. The others banged their fists against it, hoping to find a way out.

"Okay, it let us in, but it clearly doesn't want to let us out," Kristoff observed.

"And . . . we are locked in here. Probably should have seen that coming," Anna added.

Elsa sighed and let her hands drop to her sides. She decided to accept that going back through the mist wasn't the way out. When she turned to see where they had been deposited, she realized they were in the middle of the Enchanted Forest.

"This forest is beautiful," she said in awe as she stepped forward.

The others turned to see what Elsa was talking about. The most amazing, picture-perfect forest stretched before them. They kept moving, captivated by the vibrant reds and yellows of the leaves. Elsa was amazed by the forest canopy that stretched into the mist-covered sky. Sven darted from one tree to the next, scratching his back on the strong trunks.

Anna's breath caught in her throat when she stepped over a rise and looked down at the dam her father had described to her and Elsa when they were children. It was covered in vines and other shrubbery, but it was tall and vast, and no water leaked through.

"The dam. It still stands," she said. "It was in Grand Pabbie's visions. But why?"

Kristoff walked over to her. "Still in good shape . . . thank goodness."

"What do you mean?" Anna asked, looking up at him.

"Well, if that dam broke," Kristoff warned, "it would send a tidal wave so big, it would wash away everything on this fjord."

Anna couldn't hide her worry. "Everything? Arendelle's on this fjord."

"Nothing's gonna happen to Arendelle, Anna," Kristoff assured her. "It's going to be fine. Come here." He wrapped an arm around her shoulders. She leaned in close to his touch and was able to relax. Together, they gazed at the beautiful dam.

Kristoff realized how majestic everything was around them. And he had an idea.

"You know, under different circumstances, this would be a pretty romantic place . . . don't you think?"

"Different circumstances?" Anna asked, looking puzzled. "You mean like with someone else?"

"What? No, no—" Kristoff said, fishing a hand into his back pocket for the ring he had already tried to give her twice. But now seemed a better time than ever. He found it, pulled it out of his pocket, and put it behind his back. "I'm saying . . ." He cleared his throat to make sure the words came out right. "Just in case we don't make it out of here—"

Anna pulled away from him. "Wait, what? You don't think we're going to make it out of here?"

"No. No!" he said. "I mean, we *will* make it out here. Well, technically, the odds are kinda complicated. But my point is, in case we die—"

"You think we're going to die?" Anna asked, her voice getting higher.

"No!" Kristoff insisted. "No, no, no, we will die at some point, but not at any recent time will we die—"

Anna realized Elsa wasn't with them. If they were in danger, they all needed to stay together. And Anna had made an oath to Grand Pabbie to protect her sister.

"Where's Elsa?" she asked. "I swore I wouldn't leave her side. Elsa?" Anna ran off to search for her.

"—but way far in the future, we will die!" Kristoff sighed. Why couldn't he ever get it right? He'd blown it yet again. Then, as best friends do, Sven came to his side. The reindeer nudged him.

Kristoff looked at him. "Sven, don't patronize me." Kristoff felt bad enough already.

Elsa wandered among the tall trees, enjoying the beauty around her. She took in a deep, peaceful breath and closed her eyes, trying to forget her cares. But there was something . . . something she couldn't put her finger on, and it made the hairs on the back of her neck stand up. Her eyes shot open, and she spun quickly when she sensed something rushing toward her.

She was surprised to see it was Anna.

"Elsa!" her sister said. "There you are. You okay?"

"I'm fine," Elsa replied, unsettled by what she had just felt.

Anna was relieved. She took a moment to look around. "Okay. Good. Where's Olaf?"

CHAPTER 17

Olaf was happy to explore the forest. He didn't even know he was lost. He marched along, thinking his friends were right behind him.

"Anyone else feel like we're being watched. Anyone? No one?" Olaf turned around and saw only the forest. "I'm alone."

He peered deeper into the woods, trying to confirm that no one was with him.

"Anna? Elsa? Sven? Samantha?" He laughed. "I don't even know a Samantha."

He continued laughing until a gust of wind blew at his backside.

"Whoa," he said in surprise. He spun around again,

searching for the culprit. Seeing nothing, the snowman simply shrugged.

The trees above him crackled, and a pile of leaves crashed on his head. Olaf pushed the leaves off and picked one out of his mouth.

"That's normal," he said.

A rock flew out of the bushes as if from nowhere, and when Olaf turned to continue on his journey, he tripped over it and landed on his face.

A hot gush of water pushed him back up to his feet.

This is getting weird, he thought.

Tree limbs shimmied above his head, rattling the leaves as something large scampered through them. Olaf turned quickly to look behind him.

"What was that?" he asked.

A large hole gaped in the ground before him, and he quickly stopped before he fell in. He cautiously looked into what seemed to be a bottomless pit.

"Samantha?" he called, his voice echoing as it faded into the nothingness.

No response. Olaf backed away nervously.

The snowman was confident that although there was no explanation at the moment, there would be one day. He just needed to be a bit older and wiser. Then, when he thought back about everything strange that was happening to him now, he would realize it had all been completely normal.

A sizzling sound caught his attention, and he turned his head just in time to see a smoking blaze burn through the moss and race toward him. He didn't know what it was, but he knew it couldn't be good. He dove out of the way.

Olaf kept moving and soon reached a dark part of the forest, overgrown with vines and twisted branches all around him. He convinced himself that the fear he felt would seem childish in a couple of years. Creepy, unblinking white eyes peered out of the bushes everywhere he looked. He tried not to think about anything but using his manners.

"Excuse me," he said, backing out of the small grove of trees.

Olaf scurried away and found himself in a small clearing by a brook. He knew he'd make it somewhere safe! He had been willing to face his fears, and look what had happened! Olaf believed that by looking down at his reflection in the water, he would feel even better. What he saw was a distorted, rippling version of himself, but Olaf remained secure. Even with the creepy face and eyes staring back at him, nothing could shake his courage— until that image was replaced by a big scary horse's face!

"AAAAAAHHHHHH!" Olaf screamed in terror. Then a nearby bush burst into flames.

Olaf continued screaming until he ran out of breath, not even noticing that the fire in the bush went out the moment he stopped screaming.

Everything went back to normal, and he reminded himself that in a few years, he would find explanations for all these strange things. Olaf wasn't even worried when he saw trees deeper in the forest bending to the ground as if they were pushed by a heavy wind.

"This is fine," he said confidently.

But it wasn't. The heavy wind found him and swept him up into the roaring storm—one piece at a time.

CHAPTER 18

Elsa, Anna, Kristoff, and Sven were able to track Olaf down when they heard him scream. They rushed toward the whirlwind, shouting for their friend.

But the wild winds wanted more than the icy man. Everyone else was swept up into the vortex with him. The gusts whipped their bodies around in circles, arms grabbing and legs kicking as they tried to find something stable to hold on to. Anna and Elsa reached for each other as Olaf's body parts swung around them—first his midsection, then his head. "Hey, guys!" Olaf said, and then his feet passed, too. "Meet the Wind Spirit."

"Coming through," Kristoff said as he swept past Elsa.

Anna's skirt blew over her head and her hands were pulled from Elsa's grasp. Anna spun wildly out of control.

"I think I'm going to be sick!" she said.

"I'd hold your hair back, but I can't find my arms!" Olaf shouted as he sailed past her again.

Kristoff and Sven slammed into each other. They all soared higher into the vortex, flailing and flapping, grumbling and groaning. Their bodies moved forward and back, up and down. Everyone looked like they were doing a ridiculous dance.

But it wasn't just the friends who were caught in the whirlwind—the debris that had been on the forest floor was everywhere. One large tree branch soared through the vortex, headed straight for Anna. Elsa threw out her hands and hit the branch with an icy blast right before it hit her sister. The queen's magic knocked the branch free of the wind's grasp. After that, things seemed to change. The vortex centered itself on Elsa's hands.

"Hey, stop!" she said, just before it pushed the others, including all of Olaf's parts.

Kristoff landed on a mound of star moss, which cushioned his fall. Olaf's body parts fell back together in one piece on the end of log. But there was a problem. They were in the wrong order.

Sven dropped out of the sky on the other end of the log, and when he did, Olaf's parts flew back up into the air. When they came down this time, everything was exactly where it was supposed to be!

Anna fell with a splash into the brook Olaf had discovered earlier. But before she could get her bearings, a small ripple that turned into a wave rushed toward her. Anna was so frantic to get back to her sister that she didn't even notice. She jumped to her feet and moved to the bank of the brook. When she emerged on the shoreline, she began to run.

"Elsa!" she called out, never noticing watchful eyes staring at her from the crest of the small wave. "Let her go!" Anna demanded of the Wind Spirit.

Anna arrived near the vortex as Kristoff climbed out of the star moss, trying to pull off the green bits of shrubbery that clung to him.

"Anna, be careful!" he called. They tried to get close to the vortex, but it wouldn't let them in—it threw them back.

"That's my sister!" Anna shouted.

Elsa could see her friends through the rushing winds, and she knew they were doing their best to help her. She also knew she had only one option left as the vortex swirled around her, refusing to let her out.

Elsa moved her hands away from each other, as far as she could, and made a steady stream of snow to mix with the wind.

The vortex thickened with the snow's weight, which slowed the spin Elsa was in. She was sure she heard human voices, the sounds of animals, and echoes of the forest around her as the spinning continued to slow.

"Prince Agnarr!" she heard a man yell.

She closed her eyes and curled up as the slushy, ribbony whiteness overtook her. Without warning, Elsa threw open her arms, releasing all her magic, flooding the vortex with her power.

"For Arendelle," a deep voice intoned as a blast of snow filled the air with white.

CHAPTER 19

The vortex had disappeared and peace was restored to the Enchanted Forest. As the snow slowly fell from the air, Anna looked around frantically for her sister. Then she saw Elsa standing in what looked to be a garden, surrounded by beautiful sculptures made from ice. The queen looked from one sculpture to the next, stunned. Anna went to her side, taking Elsa's hand.

"Are you okay?" she asked.

Elsa squeezed her hand. "I'm fine," she said.

"What are these?" Kristoff asked when he arrived. Awestruck, he circled the ice sculptures with the rest of the group, looking closely at the detail, the delicacy.

As an ice harvester, he was a big fan of anything made of ice.

"They look like moments in time," Elsa said softly.

Elsa's words reminded Anna of something she had heard earlier. Anna turned to the snowman. "What's that thing you say, Olaf?"

"Oh!" he replied. "My theory about advancing technology as both our savior and our doom?"

"No, not the . . . not that one," Anna said. "The one about—"

"The one about cucumbers?" Olaf asked. He had read so many books and had learned so much, there were hundreds of things he had talked about to anyone who would listen.

"No, the thing about water," Anna said, narrowing it down.

"Oh, yeah," Olaf said. "Water has memory. The water that makes up you and me has passed through at least four or five people or animals before us."

Sven's head jerked up at Olaf's statement. His eyes were wide, his muzzle twisted in what appeared to be disgust. He glanced at the ice sculpture he had been licking and spit on the ground.

"It remembers everything," Olaf finished.

The wind rustled the leaves, coming from nowhere

and sweeping around Olaf. "Oh, the wind's back," he said. "I think I'll name you . . . Gale."

Everyone braced themselves as the wind moved around Anna and then slipped up the leg of Kristoff's pants.

"Ooh, ah," Kristoff called, dancing around a bit, hoping it would leave him alone. "Whoa, get out of there."

The Wind Spirit twirled in Anna's hair and made her clothing flutter as if it was examining her. "Oh, aren't you curious. . . ."

Then it moved on to Elsa and swept her up in its grip. "Oh!" she gasped. But she quickly realized the Wind Spirit was no longer being aggressive.

The group immediately stood around her, ready to protect her.

"I'm okay. I'm okay," she told them.

Gale held Elsa aloft for only a few moments before setting her gently on her feet. Elsa smiled. The Wind Spirit's energy had lifted her mood and made her feel ready to take on any obstacle that came her way.

"Did you want me to make these?" Elsa asked. The wind ruffled her skirts while she looked at the nearest ice sculpture.

But Gale didn't answer. The Wind Spirit swirled around the sisters, then swept down through a small opening in the trees. Aloft in its breeze were leaves of red and orange hues, making it easy for the group to follow where it led. Anna passed though the opening with the others. Gale had brought them to an ice sculpture that was set apart from the rest.

The sculpture depicted a couple swept up in a windstorm—a young girl helping a young boy.

Anna and Elsa approached the sculpture in disbelief. They moved around it, looking closely from every angle.

"Father?" Anna asked softly, recognizing the elements of the sculpture's face. "That's Father."

CHAPTER 20

Elsa leaned closer to the young boy and nodded. It was definitely her father. She turned her focus to the girl holding him. There was something special about her, too.

"This girl," she said.

"She's saving him . . . ," Olaf said.

"She's Northuldra," Kristoff added, recognizing that she wasn't dressed in typical Arendellian clothing.

Suddenly, a whirring sound swished from the trees closest to them. Olaf squealed and hid behind Anna. He reached into her satchel and pulled Iduna's scarf out far enough that he could wrap it over his head and shoulders, as if it could conceal him from whatever was coming their way.

"What is that?" Anna asked.

"Olaf, get behind me," Elsa ordered.

Loud bangs joined the whirring, creating a rhythmic beat. The noise filled the air, escalating in volume and tempo.

The bushes in front of them, next to the sculpture, rustled. Anna had had enough. Since they'd entered the Enchanted Forest, their experience had been anything but enchanting. Stepping forward, she reached toward another ice sculpture and broke off a sword.

"What are you going to do with that?" Kristoff asked as the whirring intensified.

"I have no idea," Anna said. But then she made a decision. Holding the ice sword in front of her, she marched toward the bushes that had since stopped moving.

With one swing, Anna cut the offensive bush down the middle. It was time to reveal whatever danger lurked within! Then she saw a group of people crouched low to the ground. Behind them stood a group of reindeer. *Are they Northuldra?* Anna thought as she stared at their unfamiliar clothes.

THUMP!

Anna spun at the loud sound. More Northuldra dropped from the trees. Each person was swinging a round object on a string, which she saw was making the whirring noise.

"Lower your weapon," a young woman commanded. She was one of the Northuldra who'd dropped from the trees. With a raised staff, she moved toward Anna and her friends. The other Northuldra moved behind her.

Swords slammed against shields. Five newcomers appeared, looking different from the Northuldra, their swords at the ready.

"And YOU lower yours," the soldier in charge commanded the Northuldra. He stood strong in a uniform that showed the wear and tear of many years. But it was still clearly an Arendellian uniform. He looked familiar to Anna.

"Arendellian soldiers?" Anna asked her friends, wondering if it was possible. She had always assumed that when the mist had closed around the forest, the only people who'd been trapped within had been their enemies, the Northuldra.

An older woman seemed to come from nowhere just then. She stood at the soldier's side, holding a staff. The soldier closed his eyes briefly, then opened them again and stared straight ahead.

"Threatening my people again, Lieutenant?" the woman said.

He regarded her like an old neighbor he had been squabbling with for years.

"Invading my dance space again, Yelana?" he responded.

The two continued to bicker like old enemies, or friends—it was hard to tell which.

"Why does that soldier look so familiar?" Anna wondered aloud. She stared at the Arendellian soldier in charge and stepped forward with the ice sword still in her hand.

A soldier noticed Anna moving toward them and shouted, "Look out, Lieutenant!"

The lieutenant spun his shield, trying to knock Yelana's staff away from his side. But Yelana countered his move.

"Get the sword!" he ordered his soldiers.

They charged Elsa, Anna, Olaf, Kristoff, and Sven. The Northuldra were close behind.

Elsa blasted her power at the ground to create a slick, glassy coating around her group. The soldiers and the Northuldra slipped and slid until they all fell onto their backs and rear ends.

The lieutenant crashed next to Yelana. "That was magic," he said in shock. "Did you see that?"

"Of course I saw it," she replied. She'd hidden her surprise.

Elsa and her friends stared at the two groups, now sprawled on the ground.

Anna leaned into her sister. "You chose a nice, cold greeting," she said.

"They've been trapped in here this whole time?" Kristoff whispered in disbelief.

"What do we do now?" Elsa whispered back.

CHAPTER 21

The history between the two groups in the forest was complicated. They'd met at the celebration for the dam completion. And that was the day they'd become enemies.

But Mattias had met Yelana long before then, during the negotiations on the cliff between the Northuldra ruler and King Runeard. He didn't need to be reminded how they were stuck in the forest. And Mattias woke every night in a cold sweat, remembering the day more than thirty-four years ago when his whole life had changed.

Boulders had fallen from the sky with perfect aim. Fire had chased the soldiers and the Northuldra like a pack of hungry wolves. Many men and women were injured, and others were lost. Mattias had been in battles before, but never one without an enemy to fight. That wasn't what bothered him the most, though. He had failed to protect the one person he'd thought of as his son: Prince Agnarr.

Mattias and his soldiers had searched the forest for days for Agnarr. Even now, he didn't want to accept that the prince had been lost forever the day the forest fell. Mattias still held out hope that somehow, Agnarr had escaped.

Mattias and Yelana had called a truce in the early years so they could work together. They had to find a way to get through the mist that had trapped them in the forest. They knew it would be better to partner in some ways, rather than to be stuck together as enemies. They didn't always get along, but there were times when they respected each other.

The soldiers had been forced to become experts at using their swords to hunt. They created bows and arrows from sticks and rope. They gathered berries, acorns, and nettles to supplement their diet. They didn't share food with the Northuldra. And the Northuldra didn't share their food with them.

Mattias had volunteered when the soldiers constructed a catapult to fire something at the mist that first week. They didn't know whether it was safe on the other side, but Mattias had been willing to give it a try. He remembered the exhilaration he'd felt when his soldiers had chopped the twisted ropes that held the catapult down. He'd laughed as he soared through the air.

But his laughter changed to dread when he bounced off the mist, as if he'd hit an invisible wall. His body flew back and crashed in a heap on the ground. The fall left him with a heavily sprained arm that never worked properly again. Just thinking about it made Mattias rub his shoulder.

The soldiers tested the catapult repeatedly over the next few months. A hammock was created to catch them when they bounced off the invisible wall. The volunteers were launched into different areas each time, but the results were always the same.

"Hey, Yelana," Mattias had called out one day.

"Yeah?" she answered.

"Four months, two weeks, and three days," he said with a wink.

"What's that?" she asked, confused.

"It's how long we've been here," he confirmed.

She shook her head. "Don't remind me."

Yelana and the Northuldra had later come up with the idea of tunneling underneath the mist. Mattias had thought it was a great plan. The Northuldra had provided them all with shovels made of wood and bone, and both sides had dug day and night for months. For years. But just like the invisible wall above the mist, there was one below the mist. Their shovels bounced off it every time.

"Hey, Mattias," Yelana had crowed after some time had passed.

"Yes, ma'am?" he asked.

"Three years, seven months, one week, and two days."

He chuckled. "Don't remind me."

A soldier had once tried to chop his way through the mist with an ax. The ax had bounced back and flown out of his hand. Mattias had moved out of the way just as it sailed past his head.

The two groups had refused to give up. Again, the soldiers and Northuldra had worked together as areas of the mist were zoned for testing with axes. Only one person at a time had been allowed in each area, and every inch of the mist was tested for a weak spot. This had taken many years and caused many injuries. No signs of weakness in the mist were ever found.

"Hey, Yelana!" Mattias had hollered at one point after receiving another ax scrape.

"What?" she asked in an annoyed voice.

"Seventeen years, eight months, three weeks, and five days."

She laughed and walked away.

The Northuldra were experts at climbing trees and mountains. Yelana had led them to the highest points to see how far up the invisible wall extended, but it didn't matter how high they went, even up to the clouds. Whenever they reached their hands out, their hands would always bounce back.

"Hey, Mattias," Yelana had growled after even more time had passed.

"I know, I know," he said with his hands up. "Twenty-four years, ten months, two weeks, and one day."

Yelana stared back at Mattias and wondered how he could be so naive. He had been there when King Runeard had arrived and promised her people friendship and cooperation. Together, they were supposed to have built a new world of greatness.

She'd seen through the lies. She'd seen the way King Runeard had looked at her people, as if he was better than them. When the children had danced and played with the magic of wind and fire, he had shaken his head and frowned. She could sense his hatred. But their leader had wanted to see the best in their new allies. He'd blindly agreed to their terms and let them in.

Yelana didn't understand why Mattias believed that nature had rewarded Elsa with magic. She felt sorry for him. Maybe he didn't know any better and really believed he'd served a great king.

Yelana had never fully trusted him or any of the soldiers, but she had been willing to work with them so she could keep them close. She'd instructed her people to stay away from the soldiers during any other times—they'd interacted only when sharing tools and ideas to escape the mist. She alone had dealt with Mattias directly.

As the years passed, Mattias truly seemed to accept her people and want to help. But Yelana had always remembered how she had thought King Runeard had seemed like a good man, too. And with him she'd made a mistake—one she would never make again.

CHAPTER 22

"I got this," Olaf said confidently as he moved out from behind Elsa and waddled forward. "Hi, I'm Olaf."

The Northuldra and Arendellians alike screamed, shouted, and slipped as they attempted to get away from the walking, talking snowman.

Olaf looked down at himself, and then back up at the frightened people. "Oh, sorry," he said. "Yeah, I just find clothes restricting. But you're wondering who we are and why we're here."

As if he were on a stage, performing a one-snowman show under a spotlight, Olaf started his dramatization.

"It began with two sisters. One born with magical powers. One born powerless."

The Northuldra and the Arendellian soldiers stared.

"Anna, no! Too high! BLAST!" Olaf fell to the ground, then quickly got back to his feet and channeled Elsa. "NO! Mama, Papa, HELP!"

Mattias looked on as the snowman continued to act out key moments in the sisters' lives.

"SLAM! Doors shutting everywhere! Sisters torn apart!"

Olaf walked around, taking on the gait and mannerisms of each person he was portraying.

"Well, at least they have their parents," Olaf said in a soft voice. Then his voice changed and became completely void of emotion: "Their parents are dead."

Next, he dramatized Elsa's little sister.

"Hi, I'm Anna. I'll marry a man I just met."

Anna wanted to melt into the ground. Although no one there knew who she was, it felt as if they had all been clued in on her biggest, most horrifying secret. She mentally prodded Olaf to move on to another subject.

"Elsa's gonna blow!" Olaf shouted. "Snow! Snow! AAHHH! Run!"

Olaf began to hum a wildly off-tune melody that seemed as if it should have been majestic.

"Magic pulses through my snowflakes," he said, and then pulled in a deep breath of air before shouting, "I live!" He held his twig arms over his head.

He took a stroll, gesturing like Elsa did when she made magical creations.

"Ice palace for one, ice palace for one. Get out, Anna! *Pew, pew!*"

Olaf spun around and staggered in what Anna felt was a completely fabricated performance.

"*My heart!*" he gasped.

Mattias's eyes widened. "Oh my goodness. . . ."

"Only an act of true love can save you," Olaf continued, his voice deepening as he did what he thought was a spot-on impersonation of Grand Pabbie.

Kristoff clapped, but after a look from Anna, he let his hands drop to his sides.

"Here's a true-love's kiss. You're not worth it. Guess what? I'm the bad guy!" Olaf exclaimed, as Hans.

"What?" Mattias shouted.

"Then Anna freezes to death . . . forever."

Mattias wiped at the tears that sprang to his eyes. "Oh, Anna."

"Then she unfreezes!" Olaf shouted. The snowman took a big breath and finished his story. "Oh, and then Elsa woke up the magical spirits, and we were forced out of our kingdom. Now our only hope is to find the truth about the past, but we don't have a clue how to do that. Except Elsa's hearing voices. So we got that going for us. Any questions?"

The Northuldra and the Arendellians had long since stopped trying to flee. They sat where they had fallen, transfixed both by the tale and the living snowman. No one knew how to react . . . to either.

"I think they got it," Olaf whispered loudly to Anna and Elsa.

With one motion of her hands, Elsa wiped away the ice on the ground. The lieutenant took his time getting to his feet. And when he did, he offered his hand to Yelana. The Northuldra woman frowned at him but accepted his help nonetheless. As soon as she stood, they parted, as if the assistance had never happened.

"Are you really Queen of Arendelle?" Mattias asked as they approached the sisters.

"I am," Elsa said.

"Why would nature reward a person of Arendelle with magic?" Yelana asked, her expression showing her confusion.

"Perhaps to make up for the actions of your people," Mattias responded as he turned to face her.

Yelana's eyes hardened. "My people are innocent. We would never attack first."

Anna and Elsa watched the decades-old enemies rehash an argument they seemed to have had many times before. But it still bothered Anna that she couldn't recall where she knew Mattias from. She framed the lieutenant's face with her fingers, making a square. She closed one eye and looked through the square at him, changing the angle and size of the square as well as her position.

"May the truth be found," he said. Then he caught sight of Anna. "Hi. I'm sorry. What's happening?"

Anna didn't answer, too intent on her task.

"This is different," he said.

"To the left," Anna instructed. "Right."

"Okay . . . this?" he asked, trying to follow her directions. "This side?"

"No, left," she corrected him.

"Sure?" Mattias moved again. "Ugh."

"Now look like you have just a little bit of indigestion," she said.

Mattias made one last move.

"That's it!" Anna shouted in excitement, causing a few people nearby to jump at her sudden burst of energy. "Lieutenant Mattias! Library, second portrait on the right! You were our father's official guard."

Mattias's eyes narrowed as what Anna was saying sank into his head. Then he looked right at her, and at Elsa, who had walked up behind her sister. He suddenly realized who the two of them were. "Agnarr . . . he was lost at sea?"

"Yes," Anna said, sadness creeping into her voice, as

it always did when she thought about the loss of her parents. "Our parents' ship went down in the Southern Sea six years ago."

The four Arendellian soldiers and Mattias bowed their heads out of respect to their fallen king and queen. When Mattias looked up, he regarded the sisters with compassion.

"I see him," he said, looking back and forth between the two of them. "I see him in your faces."

Anna was flattered to hear his words. She looked at her sister, gauging her excitement before meeting Mattias's gaze. She was thrilled to know she reminded someone of her father.

"Really?" said Anna. "He'd have been so happy to know you're okay."

"Soldiers," Mattias commanded with a signal.

The soldiers and shield maiden fell into a formation behind Elsa. They had recognized her as their queen, and with their formal military stance, they offered their support. But the atmosphere of the camp shifted dramatically when the Arendellians moved into formation. The Northuldra whispered and paced nervously, even though Mattias smiled at Yelana. Elsa felt the discomfort as well as saw it.

"Please," said Elsa, her tone soothing as she tried to calm them all. "Someone called me here. If I can just find them, I believe they have answers that may help free this forest." Elsa smiled, hoping her words would raise everyone's spirits. "Trust me, I just want to help."

But the Northuldra had trusted before, and it had been to their detriment.

"We only trust nature," said Yelana. "When nature speaks—"

Yelana was interrupted by a fireball shooting up behind Elsa, catching the leaves of a tree on fire.

Yelana waited a beat, then finished. "We listen."

CHAPTER 23

Suddenly, a bright flash of fire whipped out from behind a nearby tree in a blur, then vanished as quickly as it had appeared. Everyone stood on guard, looking around, trying to see where it had gone.

BOOM!

The tree it had come from behind lit up, blazing with flames.

"FIRE SPIRIT!" Yelana shouted.

Olaf backed away. While he didn't know what a Fire Spirit was, and even though he was now made of permafrost, he was still aware that it wasn't a good idea to be too close to fire. But this fire looked different from any he had ever seen. The flames weren't purely red and orange—Olaf saw hints of purple, too. And the flames were as terrifying as they were fascinating.

"This will all make sense when I am older," Olaf said to himself.

"Get back, everyone!" Yelana ordered, wanting nothing more than to keep her people safe.

All around, the Northuldra grabbed their children and their essentials, trying to keep away from the fire as much as they could.

"Head for the river!" Mattias yelled.

The Fire Spirit began to move, leaving a trail of the magical fire in its wake. There appeared to be no logic to its direction. Arendellians and the Northuldra ran around in confusion, having no idea which way the fire trail would go. Elsa raced after them, wanting to help any way she could.

The trail sparked and popped in the dry brush, and stray flames began new paths of their own. Flames sped up a shrub, then a tree. They appeared in the grasses. They consumed and the fire grew, taking on a life of its own.

The heat and the crackling flames added to the confusion. The Northuldra reindeer pawed the ground nervously. One of them panicked and ran off. The rest of them followed, their hooves thundering as they galloped past.

"No, no, no! The reindeer!" a Northuldra man named Ryder shouted as their movement caught his attention. "That's a dead end!"

Kristoff turned and saw that the reindeer had bolted out of the area, and he knew there wasn't any time to waste. "Come on, Sven. We'll get them!" With a quick leap, he hopped on Sven and they raced after the runaway reindeer, even as fire threatened to close their path.

But Elsa saw what was happening. She spun around and blasted her ice, widening the opening through the fire in front of them. Kristoff and Sven leaped through it.

Anna, who had been helping the Northuldra gather up their things and get to the river, turned to find that Elsa wasn't directly behind her. Instead, her sister was in the heart of the fire, her face intent as she used her power to battle the flames.

"Elsa! Get out of there!" Anna shouted.

Anna struggled against the waves of people running for their lives as she headed closer to the flames instead of away from them. She was determined to get back to her sister.

"Elsa!" she called again.

The heat of the raging fire got stronger the closer she got to her sister, and the smoke flooded her lungs

with every breath she took. But she continued. Anna
refused to leave Elsa.

Kristoff and Sven caught up with the terrified reindeer.
They pranced and grunted nervously in a small area
where the exits were blocked by fallen trees and fire.
Their unease, and the closeness of the flames, bothered
Sven as well. Kristoff patted his neck to reassure him.
"Come on, buddy," Kristoff coaxed.

There was something about the interaction between
Sven and Kristoff that calmed the other reindeer—at
least enough that the duo was able to lead them safely
away from the flames that were starting to sprout up
at the dead end. They raced back at full speed.

Kristoff felt an urgency to make sure his friends
were safe. "We can do this. Hiya!"

One by one, the reindeer jumped through the
flaming bushes until they were safely in the clearing.
Kristoff and Sven had done it! Ryder and a few of the
other Northuldra rushed forward to care for the reindeer.
Ryder looked at Kristoff gratefully. Kristoff smiled.

Now it was time to find Anna. Kristoff looked
around the flames and smoke, searching everywhere for
a glimpse of her. When he finally found her, what he
saw terrified him.

"Anna!" Kristoff yelled, frightened for her life.

Flames surrounded Anna and were closing in. Only one person could help Kristoff save her: Elsa. She had been so busy trying to control the fire that she hadn't seen the danger her sister was in. When she finally saw the threat to Anna, she changed her tactics. *Nothing can happen to her!* Elsa thought, spinning around and throwing out her magic. She created a hole in the flames just large enough for Kristoff and Sven to get through and reach Anna.

It was getting harder and harder for Anna to breathe as she lay on the forest floor, wondering how to get to Elsa. She didn't hear the sounds of hooves and Kristoff's voice. She didn't even know they were there until Kristoff grabbed her, swung her up onto Sven, and the three of them exited the same way that Sven and Kristoff had come in.

"Get her out of here!" Elsa shouted. She had been filled with fear, knowing all she could do was watch as Kristoff went after Anna. Now that her sister was safe, she wanted her to run.

"No, Elsa!" Anna cried, her voice hoarse from the smoke. They couldn't just leave her sister behind! But Kristoff didn't stop, and neither did Sven. The fire had been too close to Anna, and they wouldn't let anything happen to her.

Elsa ran toward the flames. She hadn't even heard Anna call after her. It was up to HER to put out the fire, and she would do whatever she could to stop it.

The inferno tore through the Northuldra camp, relentless and unforgiving. Elsa fought to control as much of the damage as possible. And then she saw it . . . the fireball that had started everything. It danced, it darted, it circled, and she followed it. She had been blasting the flames it had left behind, and they hadn't gone out, at least not all the way. She hadn't been able to make a dent in the blaze. It was time for a new plan.

CHAPTER 24

Elsa threw the full force of her powers on the fireball's blazing trail. She chased it until it was contained beneath a rocky overhang, where the flames seemed to lessen.

Curious, Elsa bent down and studied what was left of the fire. Two tiny, terrified eyes stared up at her. *This is the Fire Spirit?* she asked herself. *The powerful, fearsome Fire Spirit?* It looked just like a little salamander. But if anyone knew that appearances could be deceiving, it was Elsa.

The salamander whimpered, and a blast of fire shot from its mouth, aimed directly at a tree behind Elsa. But she was quick, and she froze the fire in midair, creating a spectacular display that hung there for the briefest of moments and was gone. The salamander looked from their joint creation and back to her. With one webbed foot raised, it took a hesitant step toward Elsa, moving ever so slowly, like a frightened puppy.

Elsa was deeply touched. She wondered if the creature had been hurt in the past, or misunderstood. Those were feelings she could easily relate to. She crouched down closer to the rock and leaned in, then stretched a hand out to the Fire Spirit.

The salamander slowly came forward and climbed onto her hand. It appeared to be relieved by the touch of Elsa's cold skin, making itself comfortable as it settled in, sizzling on her palm.

"Oh!" Elsa yelped in surprise. "Ow, ow." She winced from the salamander's heat, but the most important thing was for the creature to feel safe.

A thought came to her. She created snowflakes on the tips of her fingers and let them drift down to the Fire Spirit. The salamander looked at them curiously before darting out its tongue and catching them. As the Fire Spirit ate them, the flames on its back eased and the fire in the trees around them lessened. It playfully shot out a tiny burst of fire to pop another snowflake, then snuggled in the crevices of Elsa's hand. The fire went out in the other areas of the forest.

Footsteps crept up behind Elsa. She sighed. The moments she had just shared with the Fire Spirit had been so . . . magical.

"They're all looking at us, aren't they?" she whispered to her new friend.

She turned her head and glanced over her shoulder. A crowd stood about five feet away, looking and whispering. More people were approaching, many of them with their eyes wide in amazement.

"Got any advice?" Elsa whispered to the Fire Spirit, who stared at her unblinkingly. "No? Nothing?" The Fire Spirit licked its eye. "Hmm, should I know what that means?"

Then the mysterious voice broke through, haunting and eerie, pushing to the front of everything that was happening. It became the only thing Elsa could focus on. And she noticed that for the first time, someone else was focused on it, too.

The Fire Spirit looked around, searching for the source of the voice. And then just as quickly as it had begun, it stopped. Elsa turned to her friend. "You hear it, too?" she asked. "Somebody's calling us. Who is it? What do we do?" The salamander hopped out of her hand and ran up a rock, its head angled to look at something far in the distance. Then the Fire Spirit turned back to her.

"Okay, keep going north," Elsa interpreted. The salamander glowed bright for a moment, then disappeared over the top of the rock.

"Elsa!"

She turned at the sound of her sister's voice, and the smile that crossed her face when Anna appeared was brilliant. Elsa moved toward her and wrapped her arms around her little sister, relieved that she was okay.

"Oh, thank goodness," Anna said, hugging Elsa back just as tightly.

"Anna," Elsa reprimanded. Now that she knew her sister was safe, she was angry that Anna had been foolish to not get to a safe part of the forest with the others. She pulled away and frowned. "What were you doing? You could have been killed. You can't just follow me into fire."

"You don't want me to follow you into fire," Anna argued, "then don't run into fire! You're not being careful, Elsa."

Elsa took a deep breath and actually heard the words Anna said. That helped her calm down. Anna always had her best interests in mind, and she would have done the same thing. "I'm sorry. Are you okay?"

"I've been better," Anna responded.

Kristoff and Olaf remained silent as they came up behind the girls with Sven. It was not the time or place for them to interrupt. But they had never seen the girls fight before, and their concern was evident on their faces.

"Hmm, I know what you need." Elsa reached for the satchel that Anna carried and tugged on the corner of their mother's scarf dangling from the side. She pulled it out of the bag and wrapped it around her sister's shoulders.

The Northuldra around them gasped, turning to one another and whispering. Yelana moved through the crowd, approaching Elsa and Anna before raising a hand as a signal for everyone to calm down. Anna and Elsa turned to them, wondering why everyone was staring.

"Where did you get that scarf?" Yelana asked.

A young Northuldra man and woman moved closer. They seemed curious to hear the answer to Yelana's question. Anna stared at the young woman until it hit her . . . she was the one who had challenged them initially, with her staff. They nodded to each other in greeting.

"I'm Honeymaren," she said. "And that is my brother, Ryder."

Ryder stepped forward—with a smile, but also with curiosity all over his face. "That's a Northuldra scarf," he said.

CHAPTER 25

"What?" Anna asked in surprise.

"Scarves like these," Honeymaren said, gesturing to the scarf that Anna wore, "were given to a child at birth. This is from one of our oldest families."

Anna and Elsa stared at one another, both feeling overwhelmed. "It was our mother's," Anna said.

Elsa had an idea coming to her. She grabbed her sister's hand and pulled her through the brush. The others followed, wondering where they were going. The sisters rushed up to the ice sculpture of the young Northuldra girl holding their father as a boy.

"Elsa . . . ," Anna said as she touched the icy face of the girl and the scarf she wore.

Elsa examined the sculpture more closely. "I see it. That's Mother."

They turned to each other, a realization hitting them. "Mother saved father's life that day," Anna said, announcing the truth for the very first time.

After a moment, Elsa turned to Yelana, and the rest of the people gathered around them. "Our mother was Northuldra."

The silence was widespread as everyone tried to understand what they had just heard.

"What?" Mattias asked softly.

"I knew she was Northuldra," Ryder said to no one in particular. "I could just feel it. I have . . . I have a way."

And then the wind stirred through the trees, creating a harmony of nature as it wound through the leaves and branches. The ice sculptures twinkled and glistened with a magical glow, drawing everyone's attention to them. Even Olaf began to glow as the owls and animals of the night called out to the forest in song.

Olaf sang along. *"Oooohhh . . ."*

Yelana was speechless. An elder Northuldra put a hand on the shoulder of another Northuldra. That person then reached for the person in front of him and placed his hand on her shoulder. The others followed, all of them connecting with each other one by one. They began to sing a song of their people that filled the forest with a deep sense of belonging and hope.

The Arendellian soldiers stood on the outer edges, on guard. Olaf put one hand on Kristoff and the other on Sven. He wasn't exactly sure what the Northuldra were doing, but he wanted to make sure they were a part of it, too. He even sang along, though he didn't know what the words were. He was happy that the danger of the Fire Spirit was gone.

Ryder and Honeymaren were near the front of their group. They each put a hand on Yelana's shoulder. Yelana looked at Anna and Elsa. She reached for their hands and held them in her own.

"We are called Northuldra. We are the people of the sun," she said, accepting that these people were part of her family. Anna and Elsa nodded, filled with emotion.

Mattias stepped forward, seeing the feelings on their faces. He stopped and waited.

"I promise you," Elsa said to Yelana, "I will free this forest and restore Arendelle." She turned to Mattias to acknowledge him as well.

Anna was surprised by Elsa's promise. It was a vow for her sister to keep, not the two of them. Something in her stomach twisted.

"That's a pretty big promise, Elsa," she said, trying to keep the hurt to herself.

The rumble of voices started low at first, Arendellian mixing with Northuldra, then got louder as the hope of the mist falling spread through the crowd.

"We're getting out of here!" Ryder shouted, and people all around him laughed gleefully. "What! I'm excited about it!" He turned to Krisotff. "It's just . . . some of us were born in here. We've never even seen an open sky."

"Hey, I get it," Kristoff said, patting his new friend on the shoulder.

"Thanks," Ryder said. "Thank you for saving the reindeer."

"You bet," said Kristoff.

"I heard the voice again," Elsa said, smiling at Yelana. "We need to go north."

"But the Earth Giants now roam the north at night," Honeymaren warned.

"They sleep by day," Yelana advised. "You can leave in the morning."

CHAPTER 26

As everyone returned to the Northuldra camp, they were relieved to see that the damage from the Fire Spirit was not what they had imagined. Many hands tidied up in an atmosphere of celebration and thanks, relief and joy. The Northuldra and the Arendellians gathered to take a moment to recognize how important life is and how grateful they should be for each day. As music filled the air, everyone enjoyed warm drinks and bowls of steaming stew.

Near where the cooking was taking place, some of the Northuldra toddlers gathered around Olaf. At first they just looked at him curiously. He was quite different from anyone they'd ever seen before. Then one bold little girl moved forward and poked his body.

She seemed surprised that he was cold to the touch.

Olaf was thrilled to spend time with the little ones. And as they got more comfortable being around him, they drifted closer and began pulling at his arms, legs, and even at his nose. Olaf talked to them the whole time.

"Hey, let me ask you," he began, "how do you guys cope with the ever-increasing complexity of thought that comes with maturity—"

Olaf was interrupted when one of the kids grabbed his carrot nose and stuffed it up his own nose. All the kids giggled.

"Brilliant!" Olaf said. "It is so refreshing to get to talk to the youth of today. Our future is in bright hands."

But the children didn't respond with words. Some of them began to chew on him. Others took his feet off and placed them on top of his head. That made them laugh, too. Then a girl took a foot from his head and began to bite on it.

"No, no, no, don't chew that," he warned. "You don't know what I've stepped in."

Kristoff and Ryder were in a different part of the camp, near makeshift tables made from old barrels. Kristoff fumbled in his pocket and pulled out the ring he planned to give to Anna. He showed it to Ryder.

"The mountain trolls mined it out of the core of the Black Mountains," Kristoff said.

Ryder was shocked. "You know mountain trolls?"

"I was raised by mountain trolls," Kristoff announced proudly.

"Oh, I've got to get out of this forest," Ryder said. It wasn't a bad life, but he had never been out of the forest because of the mist and had always wondered what he was missing on the other side of it.

"I can't seem to get her attention," Kristoff complained, "or even say the right thing."

"Well, you're in luck; I know absolutely nothing about women, but I do know that we have the most amazing way of proposing," Ryder said. "It'll definitely get her attention. If we start now, you'll be ready by dawn."

"Really?" Kristoff asked in amazement.

Ryder grabbed his new friend's arm and pulled him. "Let's just say it involves a lot of reindeer."

Kristoff's eyes widened and he broke into a grin. "Ooohhh."

They sneaked past Anna and Mattias, who stood at the edge of the encampment eating stew. Mattias was alert, always watching, always scanning. He never seemed to let down his guard.

"He was about your height," Anna said to the

lieutenant. She was happy to stand with him and eat stew while he kept watch. She respected him because she would never have been born if he hadn't saved her father all those years before. And she was grateful that Mattias had taken such good care of her father when he was a young men. It was hard for Anna to believe that he'd been stuck in the Enchanted Forest for longer than she had been alive.

"That tall, huh," Mattias asked, thinking back to the boy he used to know. There were moments when it was hard for him to reconcile his own memories of Agnarr with the information Anna and Elsa shared with him.

"You meant a lot to him. Whenever we'd get butter biscuits from Blodgets' Bakery, he'd say, 'Mattias could never get enough of these.'"

"It's the butter . . . ," Mattias said. He had given up hope long before of ever getting back to the things he loved. But now with Anna and Elsa there in the forest . . . the hope had returned. "Hey, back at home—Halima still over at Hudson's Hearth?"

"She is," Anna said.

Mattias couldn't believe it. So many years had passed! "Really? She married?" He asked. Anna shook her head no. "Oh, wow. Why doesn't that make me feel better?"

"What else do you miss?" Anna asked.

"My father," he answered without hesitation. "He passed long before all this. He was a great man. Built us a good life in Arendelle, but taught me to never take the good for granted. He'd say, 'Be prepared—just when you think you've found your way, life will throw you onto a new path.' "

"What do you do when it does?" Anna asked.

"Don't give up," he said. "Take it one step at a time, and . . ."

"Just do the next right thing?" Anna added, remembering what Grand Pabbie had told her.

"Yeah," Matthias said with a smile. "You got it." Then he saw the concern on Anna's face as she watched Elsa walk past with Honeymaren.

CHAPTER 27

Honeymaren and Elsa walked over to the logs around a campfire and sat down. A baby reindeer ran up, nuzzling and rubbing its head on them. Elsa stroked the little reindeer's back as she thought about everything that had happened since they'd entered the forest.

"I want to show you something. May I?" Honeymaren asked. Elsa nodded. Honeymaren reached for one end of the beautiful burgundy scarf that had belonged to Elsa's mother and gestured to the snowflakes on it. She identified the symbols on the points of one snowflake. "You know air, fire, water, earth."

"Yes," Elsa said.

"But look." Honeymaren touched a diamond in the center of the snowflake, a symbol Elsa had never noticed before. "There's a fifth spirit." Honeymaren smiled at the surprised expression on Elsa's face. "Said to be a bridge between us and the magic of nature."

Elsa was shocked. "A fifth spirit?"

"Some say they heard it call out the day the forest fell," Honeymaren said. She had Elsa's full attention.

"My father heard it," said Elsa. "Do you think that's who's calling me?" Elsa asked.

"Maybe." Honeymaren smiled. "Alas, only Ahtohallan knows."

Elsa smiled back, recalling that her mother had said the same thing to Anna and herself when they were children. "Ahtohallan—" She drew the scarf tightly around her shoulders, remembering the words to the lullaby her mother had soothed them with. She half sang and half spoke the words aloud.

Honeymaren smiled again, recognizing the song and singing along with Elsa.

"Why do lullabies always have to have some terrible warning in them?" Honeymaren asked once they had finished.

"I wonder that all the time," Elsa said.

Suddenly, the ground shook from a distant boom like thunder. But no lightning followed to electrify the sky.

"Earth Giants," Honeymaren said.

CHAPTER 28

Everyone panicked and scattered in different directions. They doused the cooking fires and grabbed the children. They searched for places to hide from the looming threat.

"What are they doing down here?" Yelana whispered sharply to Elsa.

The ground shook again, as if feet the weight of mountains stomped on it. The giants were close; tree limbs wavered from their heavy breathing. A huge nose parted the limbs and sniffed loudly, searching for a specific scent.

"Hide," Honeymaren instructed.

Olaf quickly ducked behind a rock, trying to make himself as small as possible. And then he noticed the

Fire Spirit. He waved his hands at the salamander, trying to shoo it away. His gestures had the opposite effect: the Fire Spirit ignited!

He gasped in horror. "No, no, shhh," he said, trying to soothe it. Taking a deep breath, he blew on the crackling flames, but the flames expanded, engulfing the Fire Spirit. "They're coming. They're coming!"

He tried blowing on the flames again, yet they continued to spread. Olaf reached for the Fire Spirit. "Ooh. Ooh. Hot. Hot," he said as he tossed the creature back and forth between his hands. Finally, he put the salamander back down on the rock and looked at it pleadingly. "Unlight that fire," he begged.

Without warning, the Fire Spirit jumped onto Olaf's head, turning around three times before lying down on the cold permafrost with a smile. At first Olaf winced in pain. Then he gave a sigh of relief—the fire on the salamander had gone out.

BOOM, BOOM, BOOM.

Everyone in the Earth Giants' path held their breath and prayed they would just go away. Elsa, intrigued, peeked out from behind the tree. The nose of the one closest to her turned slowly toward her, as if it had caught her scent. A shadow crossed over her as the whole Earth Giant emerged. Before ducking behind the tree, she looked up at its face, intrigued by its sheer size and the velocity with which it moved toward her. Then, without warning, it turned in a different direction and continued walking.

Elsa peeked out from behind the tree again. Realizing the Earth Giant was moving away from their camp, she stepped out and started after it. Anna jumped into her path, her face full of questions.

"Tell me you were not about to follow them," she whispered.

"What if I can settle them like I did the wind and fire?" Elsa asked.

"Or what if they can crush you before you even get the chance? Remember, the goal is to find the voice, find the truth, and get us home," Anna reminded her sister.

Olaf ran up just as the Earth Giants faded into the distance. The Fire Spirit was still relaxing comfortably on his head.

"Hey, guys—that was close! But, bright side: the Fire Spirit and I are fast friends. We're going with the name Bruni. Either that or Sally. Aren't we, Bruni . . . or Sally?"

Elsa smiled and Bruni jumped onto her arm and sat on her shoulder. "Good. Watch your twigs, though, Olaf." She turned to Anna. "The giants sensed me. They may come back here. I don't want to put anyone at risk again. And you're right, Anna; we've got to find the voice. We're going now."

Anna hesitated. "Okay. We're going. Let me just—"

But Elsa didn't wait another second for her sister to finish. She went through the camp, with Olaf at her heels, determined to continue her journey north.

Anna looked around the camp. "Where are Kristoff and Sven?" she asked in a panic.

"Oh, yeah. I think they took off with that Ryder guy and a bunch of reindeer," Olaf said.

"They left?" Anna asked, confused. "Just . . . just left? Without saying anything?" *What could be so important that Kristoff would leave me behind?*

Olaf shrugged. "Who knows the ways of men?" He turned and followed Elsa.

Anna glanced back at her sister, getting farther away with each second. Anna didn't want to leave without Kristoff. But she'd promised to keep Elsa safe.

She raced off and caught up with Olaf. Elsa was ahead of them, pushing through the forest with determination, always aware of the potential dangers all around. Anna did her best to hold her head up and not cry. And when Olaf reached his hand up to her, she gladly took it.

CHAPTER 29

Kristoff was excited for the day ahead as he stood in a beautiful cove full of wildflowers, watching the sun rise. Stray sunbeams fell on his hair, highlighting the white lichen sprinkled there. He had even put some on Sven, for good luck.

"Okay," he said. "Everybody ready?"

Among the trees, reindeer surrounded Kristoff in a spiral formation.

Ryder was there, too and knew how to have fun with them. "Ready," he said in the voice of one of the reindeer.

He changed his voice again. "Um, I could use a rehearsal."

In another voice, Ryder said, "I love love."

Kristoff was shocked. "Wait. You talk for them, too?"

Ryder, not ashamed, said, "I do."

"It's like you can actually hear what they're thinking." Kristoff beamed. The reindeer looked at each other as if they thought the two men were crazy.

"Yeah," Ryder agreed.

"And then you just say it," they said simultaneously.

Kristoff was happy to have a friend who thought like him.

They stopped when the sound of footsteps broke the quiet of the morning.

"Okay," Ryder said in his real voice. "Here she comes."

Kristoff and Ryder launched into motion. They hit triggers that made flowers fly and butterflies soar in a colorful dance through the air. Kristoff hopped onto a boulder in the middle of a big circle of them. He poked one rock with his toe and it nudged the others to fall in a dazzling domino effect around him.

"Princess Anna of Arendelle, my feisty, fearless, ginger-sweet love, will you marry—" he began.

He froze when Yelana walked into the clearing. She looked around as if she had no idea what to say. "This is so sudden . . . ," she said. "Um. The princess left with the queen."

That didn't make any sense to Kristoff. Why would

Anna and Elsa leave? And more important, why would they leave without him?

"What?" asked Kristoff. "Wait, what? What?"

Yelana shrugged. The situation was getting really awkward, and she was ready to leave. She was just a messenger.

"I wouldn't try to follow," she said. "They're long gone."

Kristoff couldn't move. "Long gone?"

"Yeah," she confirmed. "So—we're heading west, to the lichen meadows. You can come with us if you want." She turned and walked out of the cove.

Kristoff was shocked. He couldn't think. He was too embarrassed to meet Ryder's eyes, knowing that Ryder knew Anna had left the Northuldra camp without even telling him. They had put so much work into this proposal because he was sure that he and Anna were meant to be together forever.

"Hey . . . ," Ryder said, feeling bad for his new friend. "I'm really sorry that—"

"No, I'm fine," Kristoff interrupted, lying.

"Yeah. Yup. Okay. I better go pack," Ryder said. "You coming with?"

"I'll just, uh— Yeah, I'll meet you there," Kristoff promised.

"Okay. You know where you're going? Right?" Ryder asked.

"Yeah," he confirmed. "Yeah. I know the woods."

Ryder nodded and headed for the camp.

Kristoff's whole body felt numb. He sat on the boulder he'd been standing on and put his head in his hands. Sven nudged him to offer support and to make sure his best friend was okay.

How could she leave me behind? Should I even follow her? Are we growing apart? Kristoff thought. He felt lost without her.

CHAPTER 30

Elsa kept a steady pace ahead of Anna and Olaf. It was hard to tell how long they had been walking, but the night had slowly slid into day as they continued moving north. Bruni ran along on the rocks beside Elsa, stopping periodically to make sure everyone was still there.

Anna could tell that her sister was anxious by the way her eyes darted back and forth, looking at everything. Elsa sang the same haunting melody that had called to her so many times, wanting it to answer back . . . wanting it to tell her which way to go. Of course, Olaf, not to be left out, tried to copy her, singing in what he thought was the same voice. But it was far from it, and it made Bruni jump into the air and catch fire. The Fire Spirit looked at Olaf grumpily before dousing its flames and scrambling off into the bushes.

The snowman's off-key singing made Anna grit her teeth, but she tried to be polite.

"Hey, Olaf—um, maybe just one of you should do it," she suggested.

"I agree," Olaf said, nodding. He raised a stick hand so he could whisper to Anna behind it. "She's a little pitchy."

A soft breeze whirled around him, announcing that the Wind Spirit had returned.

"Hey, Gale's back," Olaf said happily.

Gale fluttered around Elsa, getting her attention before drawing their eyes to a tattered flag that was barely visible over one of the hills.

"What . . . ?" Anna said, breathless.

She and Elsa hurried through the trees with Olaf right behind them. They stopped suddenly on the crest of the hill and stared in silence before grabbing each other in shock. It was an Arendellian flag—old and in pieces, and attached to the mast of a ship. The vessel lay shipwrecked and broken in a dry riverbed, its hull ripped open.

Gale swept around the girls and blew toward the

ship, pushing against the old, beaten flag, making it wave weakly.

"How can it be?" Anna asked.

Olaf studied the fragmented vessel curiously, not noticing that the girls were upset.

"What is it?" he asked.

"Mother and Father's ship," Anna replied softly, hardly believing it.

Olaf was confused. "But this isn't the Southern Sea."

"No. No, it isn't," Anna said. It didn't make any sense, and yet there it was. She ran with Elsa down the embankment, desperate to get to the ship, throwing caution behind them. They were too fast for Olaf, but he tumbled after, trying his best to keep up with them.

The broken hull was jagged, but Elsa and Anna didn't hesitate as they navigated the splintered beams and climbed into the old wooden ship. More than anything, they hoped to find something of their parents', anything they may have left behind. But their brief moment of hope was soon gone. Everything inside had been destroyed over the years—tossed and mangled, or washed away. They moved silently through the wreckage in heartbroken shock.

"*Why* is their ship here?" Elsa asked, on the verge of tears. "*How* is it here?"

They searched deeper, under jagged wooden planks and ripped sails.

"It must have been washed in from the Dark Sea," Anna guessed, sorting through the mess, her fingers moving faster and faster.

"What were they doing in the Dark Sea?" Elsa asked. She didn't expect her sister to have an answer.

"I don't know," Anna replied. She stopped and stared at Elsa. Everything felt more mysterious than it had before. "So many secrets."

Olaf's head popped up over the side of the broken beams. Seeing the girls, he pushed himself the rest of the way in and tumbled into the hull. His head swiveled as he looked around, confused.

"How did the ship get through the mist?" he said. "I thought nobody could but us. Oh . . . unless nobody was on it."

Anna needed to concentrate on her sister. "There's got to be something here . . . ," she said, refusing to believe they had come this far to find out that all the answers were still hidden. Suddenly, an idea struck her. "Wait. Wait. Look around." She dropped to her knees and felt around the floor with her hands. "Every Arendellian ship has a compartment. Waterproof."

Anna's words pushed Elsa into action. She ran

her hands over the walls, looking for any sign of a compartment.

"That's very clever," Olaf said. "Although it does make me wonder why they don't just make the whole ship waterproof."

"Here," Anna said. Her finger went into a small notch near the floor. It clicked and a hatch opened. Olaf and Elsa went to her in anticipation as Anna reached inside and pulled out a round glass tube. She uncorked it and removed a roll of parchments covered in mysterious text. "What language is this?"

"I don't know," Elsa said, glancing at some words in the margins. She pointed to them. "But look—this is Mother's handwriting."

Anna read the words out loud. "'The end of the ice age . . . The river found but lost . . . Magic's source. Elsa's source?'"

Elsa took the parchment from her and read the mention of herself.

Anna opened another parchment. "It's a map," she said. Anna unrolled it carefully and gently spread it out on the floor. Elsa joined her and they looked at it together.

The map showed Arendelle, the Enchanted Forest, the Dark Sea, and what lay beyond. A crude line marked the mist, with question marks along its northern border. Dotted lines marked a route up the fjord.

"They traveled north to the Dark Sea, to—" Anna stopped short when the dotted lines crossed the sea to a small island, labeled again in their mother's unique handwriting.

Elsa recognized the word. "Ahtohallan . . ."

"It's real?" Anna asked.

"Ahto-who-what?" Olaf asked.

"Ahtohallan," Elsa corrected him. "It's a magical river said to hold all the answers about the past."

Olaf felt proud that he had been right. "Reinforcing my water-has-memory theory—"

"Water has memory," Elsa whispered. She closed her eyes and pressed her hands to the floor. She used her power to pull moisture from the old wooden beams, the air, and the floorboards.

"Elsa?" Anna said, "What are you doing?"

"I want to know what happened to them," Elsa said.

A lacy, life-size ice sculpture formed in front of them, a perfect replica of their parents, dancing together and looking lovingly at each other. The sisters moved around it, taking in every detail.

Gale swept past them again and around the sculpture. As it swirled, echoes of distant voices filled the ship.

"*Ahtohallan has to be the source of her magic,*" said the distant, distorted voice of the girls' mother in a memory from long before.

"*If we know why Elsa has powers, we can help her,*" their father said.

Elsa had an idea. She moved through the ship and placed her hands on a wall. Another sculpture formed, a replica of her parents sitting at a table, looking over a map.

"*Do you really think the past can save Elsa's future?*" her father asked.

"*No,*" her mother replied, "*but I think understanding what she's a part of can.*"

Elsa backed away from the sculpture, realizing that all of this was about *her*. Gale swept through the ship. Elsa followed it to the helm, understanding what she was supposed to do. She put her hands on either side of the doorframe and closed her eyes.

A sculpture began to form in front of her from the ground up. It was a wave.

"They look so scared," Elsa said as Gale spun around the sculpture.

"*The waves are too high,*" Queen Iduna said.

"*We keep going for Elsa,*" King Agnarr replied as a wave crashed onto the deck. "*Iduna!*"

"*Agnarr!*" she shouted back.

"I love you!" he cried.

"I love you!" she answered.

Elsa's parents held each other as another wave overtook them. Elsa couldn't watch anymore and bolted from the ship.

"Elsa!" Anna called as she ran after her sister.

CHAPTER 31

Elsa doubled over on the dry riverbank, tears running down her face. She felt completely overwhelmed by what she had seen on the ship. She missed her parents more than ever. She had always known they had not survived, but now she had proof.

Anna came to Elsa's side, putting a hand on her back as she spoke softly to her. "Hey, hey, hey. What are you doing?"

"This is my fault," Elsa confessed, her voice choked with emotion. "They were looking for answers about me."

Anna did what she could to comfort her. "You are not responsible for their choices, Elsa."

"No, just their deaths," she lamented.

"Stop," Anna demanded. "No. Yelana asked why would the spirits reward Arendelle with a magical queen? Because our mother saved our father. She saved her enemy. Her good deed was rewarded with you. You are a gift."

Elsa looked up at her sister. "For what?" she asked softly.

"If anyone can resolve the past, if anyone can save Arendelle and free this forest, it's you," Anna explained. "I believe in you, Elsa, more than anyone or anything."

Elsa clasped Anna's hands tightly, grateful for her sister's words of encouragement. She took a moment to dry her tears as she made a decision. "Honeymaren said there was a fifth spirit, a bridge between the magic of nature and us."

"A fifth spirit?" Anna asked, surprised that Elsa hadn't told her about it before.

"That's who's been calling me . . . from Ahtohallan. The answers about the past are all there."

"So we go to Ahtohallan," Anna said.

Elsa did have a plan to go to Ahtohallan. But that plan did not involve her sister.

"Not *we. Me,*" she said.

Anna didn't like Elsa's answer at all. They were supposed to take this journey together. Grand Pabbie had entrusted her to protect Elsa, and even if he hadn't,

Anna would have never let her sister go off alone. And now to hear her say that was exactly what she wanted to do, Anna wanted answers. "What?"

"The Dark Sea is too dangerous for us both," Elsa warned.

"No," Anna insisted. "No. We do this together. Remember the song? Who will stop you from going too far?"

"You said you believed in me," Elsa reminded her. "That this is what I was born to do."

"And I don't want to stop you from that," Anna assured her. "I don't want to stop you from being whatever you need to be!" She made one last attempt to make Elsa see things her way. "I just don't want you dying . . . trying to be everything for everyone else, too. Don't do this alone. Let me help you. Please. I can't lose you, Elsa."

Elsa looked at her with weary eyes. "I can't lose you, either, Anna." She hugged her sister and motioned for Olaf to join them. "Come on," she encouraged him.

After Olaf had joined Anna, Elsa used her powers to quickly blast a small ice path that flowed along the dry riverbed.

CHAPTER 32

"Wait, what?" Anna asked, confused.

But Elsa wasn't done. Next, she created an iceboat right under Anna's and Olaf's feet. They fell back into it. Once they were seated, Elsa waved her hand to send them racing down the icy path she had created.

"What are you doing?" Anna cried. "Elsa!" She threw out her arms and did whatever she could to stop them from sliding along the ice path. "No! No! Olaf, help me stop. GIVE ME A HAND!"

He yanked one of his arms off and gave it to her. Anna stared at it, then she shook it. What was she supposed to do with it? How was it going to help them stop and get back to Elsa?

Anna spotted a tree with a low-hanging branch up ahead. "Hang on!" she said. She held up Olaf's arm and let his hand grab the branch. The boat swiveled as it changed course and flew up onto dry land. Anna and Olaf were relieved that her plan had worked!

They both breathed a sigh of relief. But neither of them had counted on the speed of their iceboat, which continued to push them over a slope and down a hill. Then they splashed into a river.

"Wait," Anna said frantically. "Wait. No. No. No!" The boat raced even faster down the river than it had down the ice path. It began to spin. "Oh, come on!" Anna shouted angrily.

"Anna," Olaf said, "this might sound crazy, but I'm sensing some rising anger."

Anna hit a tree when the boat rotated. "Argh! Well, I am angry, Olaf," Anna admitted. "She promised me we'd do this together!"

That wasn't what Olaf had meant. "Ya-huh. But what I mean is I'm sensing rising anger in *me*."

Anna paused in trying to stop the boat and gave the little snowman her full attention.

"Wait, *you're* angry?" she asked.

"Um . . . I think so?" Olaf said uncertainly. "Elsa pushed *me* away, too. And didn't even say goodbye."

Anna understood then that Olaf was just like her. "And you have every right to be very, very mad at her."

"And," he said with panic on his face. "You said some things never change, but since then everything's done nothing *but* change."

Seeing how this had affected her friend, Anna let go of her anger. "I know. But look, I'm still here holding your hand."

Olaf felt a little better. "Yeah. That's a good . . . that's a good point, Anna. But there's one more thing. Please, don't leave me, too. Your parents left you both, and we left Kristoff and Sven, and then Elsa left us . . . and if you leave, then—"

She knew he was troubled and she needed to ease his fears. "Hey, hey, hey—I'm not going to leave you, Olaf. . . . Not ever."

"Promise?" he asked.

"I promise." Anna still had the arm he had given her to try to stop the iceboat. The pinky on the hand wiggled.

"Pinky swear," he said.

"Pinky swear," she confirmed, wrapping her pinky around his and shaking it.

An odd thought occurred to Olaf. "Did you ever notice that our smallest finger contains our most positive swear power, while our longest finger contains our most nega—"

Anna slammed a hand over his mouth. "Olaf. No. Shhh!" The banks of the river were covered in sleeping Earth Giants.

He didn't see them at first. "Don't shush me. That's rude and—" Then he saw them and lowered his voice to a whisper. "Oh, the giants. . . . They're huge."

Anna and Olaf silently glided past them. Anna saw up ahead that the river split into two paths. One path was lined with Earth Giants. The other led to a waterfall.

"Hang on, Olaf," Anna said, having made a split-second decision about which way was best. "Try not to scream." She reached out and grabbed a branch that redirected them toward the waterfall and away from the giants.

Moments later, they careened down the rushing water toward a pit.

Olaf screamed.

CHAPTER 33

Anna slammed two rocks together and created a spark to light a piece of driftwood. The Lost Caverns that the waterfall had deposited them in lit up. She spotted Olaf's carrot and reached to grab it out of the water as it floated by. "Found it."

She carried the torch back to Olaf. He was putting his body back together on the shore of a pool of water. The broken iceboat and Anna's wet cloak were next to him. Anna pushed Olaf's carrot back into his face.

He spit out a fish and a mouthful of river water. "Thank you. Where are we?" he asked.

Anna looked up at the waterfall. "In a pit with no way out?"

Olaf spotted a dark opening behind a rock and

ran to it. "But with a spooky, pitch-black way in." He smiled back at her as he pointed to it.

Anna approached him and looked into the opening. She couldn't decide if it was worth the risk of whatever was inside. They could wait in the pit for help, but how would anyone ever find them down there?

Olaf grabbed her hand and gave a little tug. "Come on," he said. "It'll be fun, assuming we don't get stuck here forever, no one ever finds us, and you starve and I give up."

Anna hesitated and looked around for another way out. But after seeing nothing else, she sighed and gave Olaf a nod. She held tightly to his hand and stepped into the darkness.

"But, bright side: Elsa's gotta be doing a whole lot better than we are," Olaf said, sounding hopeful.

CHAPTER 34

Elsa stood on the shore of a dark, rocky beach that night while the wind whipped her hair around her face. The ferocious waves rose high and crashed before her on the shore like thunder. She gazed out across the waters and saw an icy landmass in the far distance. She had done it. She had made it to the Dark Sea. Now she just had to make it across.

Determined, Elsa removed her coat and boots. She released her hair from its braid and tied it behind her neck before taking a deep breath. She sprinted toward the tumbling waves. Frozen snowflakes radiated from each footfall, supporting her weight.

Twenty feet from the shoreline, the waves overtook

her, knocking her down and shattering the ice she'd made.

Elsa was not going to give up. Dripping wet, she started over. She ran full force at the sea. She got past the first set of waves by leaping onto a large rock that sat a short distance from the shore. Then she froze the seawater that crashed against the rock and used it to make a slide to gain speed for her attack on the second set of waves.

One of those waves was colossal, however. It soared high above her. Elsa tried to freeze it, but it was too powerful. The ice wall she had attempted to create crashed on top of her, plunging her beneath the surface.

In the darkness underwater, waves continued to roll overhead. Lightning flashed, brilliantly illuminating the depths of the sea around her as she headed for the surface. But when the second electrical strike lit up the sky, it also showed what appeared to be a huge, ferocious horse deep in the water below. The horse swam up and looked her in the eye. Lightning struck again and the horse, the Water Spirit, was gone.

Elsa clawed her way to the surface. Waves tossed her as she looked down to see the Water Nokk galloping up from the depths, heading straight for her. She created an ice sheet to float on top of the water's surface, and pulled herself onto it just in time for the Water Spirit to ram her vessel and send her careening into the air.

Struggling to breathe, Elsa turned to see the horse attacking again.

Its hooves drove her underwater. She tried to break free as it pushed her deeper and deeper. She grabbed onto the Water Nokk's hooves and froze the horse. It resisted, and then the Water Spirit shattered into billions of particles of ice.

Elsa swam straight up, hoping to get away before the Water Nokk re-formed itself. She reached the surface, but the horse was right there and threw her out of the water.

Lightning flashed.

Elsa created a giant ice wave that collapsed onto the Water Nokk.

Lightning flashed again.

Underwater, Elsa made an ice shield to block the horse. It burst through the shield as if nothing were there at all.

Lightning flashed once more.

Above the water, the Water Nokk grabbed Elsa's arm and dragged her through the waves. She fought to breathe. Desperate, she used her magic to throw out an ice bridle. It hooked onto the Water Spirit's mouth and head. She swung around and landed on the horse's back.

The Water Nokk panicked and bucked. But Elsa yanked on the reins and tried to gain control. The horse surfaced and turned toward the icy landmass that Elsa had seen in the distance. It ran, fighting, trying to throw her off, refusing to give in to her commanding hold.

Elsa pulled the reins tighter and pressed her legs down harder until the horse responded. Finally, its stride evened out and she relaxed her grip. They moved together, Elsa and the Water Nokk.

The icy landmass came into view ahead. It appeared to be an island. As Elsa got closer, she realized it was more than an island. It was a giant glacier that sparkled with magic. She was overwhelmed with joy.

"Of course," she whispered. "Glaciers are rivers of ice." The voice she had longed to reach called out to her, closer than ever. "Ahtohallan is frozen." All she had to do was reach the secret river.

The voice continued to call to her, filling her ears. It sounded almost joyful, as if it knew she was near.

"I hear you," Elsa said, "and I'm coming."

She snapped the reins and the Water Nokk quickened its pace.

Elsa couldn't stop trembling with anticipation as she approached Ahtohallan with the Water Spirit.

Knowing the voice that had been calling to her was there gave her comfort.

The Water Nokk turned when they reached the shore, allowing Elsa to leap onto the icy white beach. The ground shimmered when her feet landed. It was a magical response. She felt power emanating all around her. It felt like she was home.

The horse shook its mane and turned back to the Dark Sea, slowly dissipating into the water. Elsa's eyes moved from it and gazed up at the giant ice cave that stretched endlessly in front of her. She moved toward an opening in the ice that loomed like a fortress.

CHAPTER 35

Elsa shivered as she looked at the glacier ahead of her. *Ahtohallan, the secret river from Mother's lullaby. It's real,* she thought. There was something about it that seemed so . . . familiar. She wondered if the familiarity came from the calling of the voice, or from the connection of magic. Because of how the colored lights twinkled and danced around the entrance to Ahtohallan, she knew it was full of magic.

Elsa boldly stepped into the opening of the ice cave, instantly feeling like she was finally where she was meant to be. She looked around with wonder at the smooth white walls, wondering what kinds of secrets were inside Ahtohallan. Elsa was nervous, but eager to find out.

The voice continued to call to Elsa in its haunting melody, and she answered back with confidence. She had always known that the voice wanted to help her, but she'd never imagined it would lead her to Ahtohallan. She moved around the cave's entrance, following the call, willing to go where it led, ready for the voice to reveal itself. She was ready to learn.

The voice guided Elsa to a door in the ice. All she had to do was open it. The voice called to her again, stronger, and Elsa responded. Reaching out without hesitation, she pulled the door open and rushed forward, overcome with emotion and excitement for whatever lay ahead. She would do whatever it took to reach the voice. Every inch of her tingled to be with it as she dodged sharp, beautiful crystals that adorned the walls.

Elsa had never been more certain of anything in her life. She was there for a reason—and maybe it was the same reason she had been born. She was different from everyone else, and it was time to find out why. She didn't tremble anymore. She just needed the voice to show her where she belonged.

The path through the cavern was not an easy one. The voice led Elsa over pillars of ice that tumbled as she leaped from one to the next. It called her to the bottom of a deep ravine, which she reached by creating a long staircase of ice that she ran down. Elsa met every challenge and triumphed.

Finally, she found herself in a giant room with a domed roof, where memories danced along the walls and ceiling. The memories were fuzzy, unclear. Though Elsa tried as hard as she could, she couldn't make out what they were.

But the young queen could see the symbols for the spirits of nature, dancing and swirling around her. She reached for them, forming them into giant diamonds of ice. With her magic, she guided the diamonds to the floor, assembling them in the same snowflake pattern that was knitted into her mother's scarf. But one was missing: the fifth element, the bridge between nature and people. Elsa stepped into the empty space and fulfilled her destiny.

The dome above her instantly illuminated with memories, but this time they were sharp and crystal clear. Perhaps it was a reward. The voice called to her again, and Elsa knew it too was one of the memories. When she called back, the memory clarified and came forward, facing her and singing the haunting melody. It all made sense. She stepped toward it and sang alongside the memory of her mother, who, as a young girl, had called out the day the forest fell.

Elsa understood why her mother had been there.

Elsa had risked her life by moving through air, fire, water, and earth to be there. She was born for this and had proven her worth when she'd met up with the spirits of nature.

As Elsa sang along in harmony with the memory of Iduna, she began to transform into who she was always meant to be. Her dress spun around her body, and her hair fell loose and wildly untamed. A crown of vines and leaves adorned her head as the other elements swirled around her—air, fire, water, and earth. Elsa had transformed into the element Honeymaren had spoken of. *Elsa* was the fifth spirit, the bridge between nature and people. She was the Snow Queen.

CHAPTER 36

With her hands, Elsa manipulated the giant symbols suspended in the air and used them to build a new snowflake, with the elements as the branches and herself as the center. This was the version of herself that Elsa had been waiting for her entire life, and it was what the other elements had been waiting for as well.

As Elsa looked around, the memories played out in front of her. It was as if her transformation was the key that had unlocked them.

Elsa raised her arms and used her magic to draw the memories closer. They landed all around her, the icy reflections of the past. Unlike the sculptures she had made in the forest, these moved and interacted with her. The voices were as clear as if the people in the memories were there in person. At first it seemed she didn't know them, but as she looked closer, she gasped in surprise.

The first memory was of a young girl twirling high in the wind and a boy looking after her. She recognized them as her parents, on the day the Northuldra and Arendellians had fought in the forest. Her mother was riding on the currents of Gale.

Taking another step, Elsa recognized the memory that had solidified into a statue in the forest—it was her mother holding her father as she saved him. Elsa gasped when she realized why the image was suspended in the air; the Wind Spirit had lifted them out of the Enchanted Forest while others were locked in. It was Gale. Gale had always been there to protect Elsa's family, even before she was born.

Elsa walked faster as new memories appeared with every step she took. She saw her mother in an orphanage in the woods outside Arendelle. *"No one knew who you were,"* she heard. *"You didn't have any family with you."*

She passed the next memories in a hurry—there were so many to see. Anna riding by as a child, standing on the seat of her bike. The bishop announcing the day Elsa took the throne: *"Presenting Queen Elsa of Arendelle."* Elsa's mother studying old documents in the library of the castle: *"What have you found?"* asked her father. *"I think we've been looking on the wrong side of the sea,"* her mother replied.

Elsa moved through crowds while continuing to watch her family. She spotted Hans talking to Anna. *"I'm great, actually,"* she said to him. He bowed and introduced himself. *"Prince Hans of the Southern Isles."* Elsa threw a blast of power, shattering that memory, before walking on.

She watched a younger version of herself and her sister, fascinated. *"Conceal, don't feel; conceal, don't feel. . . ."* Elsa kept moving.

Anna's voice rang out: *"I love you, Olaf!"*

Elsa smiled when she saw her parents' wedding. *"To have and to hold, from this day forward—"* her father promised. Then there were her parents when they were younger. She laughed as she watched her mother drop from a tree and sit next to her father. *"Iduna,"* said Agnarr. *"What are you reading, Your Majesty?"* a teenage version of her mother asked. *"Some new Danish author,"* he said.

Elsa blasted the memory with her magic and continued walking. This time she found her parents as adults, and they were embracing. *"I need to tell you about my past, and where I am from,"* Iduna said sadly. *"I'm here,"* said Agnarr, pulling her into his arms.

Elsa felt a breeze above her and looked up. The wind carried her father and mother, young teenagers in this memory, and placed them on an Arendellian cart. She watched her mother place a blanket over her father, then drape an Arendellian cloak around herself as soldiers arrived. *"Get the prince out of here,"* a soldier said to the wagon driver.

Elsa sensed someone behind her.

"Lieutenant Mattias," a voice said. She turned to see a royal Arendellian walk by with another soldier at his side. A much younger Mattias turned at the sound of his king's voice.

"Grandfather—" Elsa whispered, seeing King Runeard for the first time.

"We bring Arendelle's full guard," the king ordered.

"But they have given us no reason not to trust them," argued Mattias.

Elsa's grandfather shook his head. *"The Northuldra follow magic, which means we can never trust them."*

His words hurt and deeply troubled Elsa. "Grandfather?" she said softly.

"Magic makes people feel too powerful, too entitled. It

makes them think they can defy the will of a king," said King Runeard firmly.

Elsa shook her head. "That is not what magic does," she said. "That's just your *fear. Fear* is what can't be trusted."

Her grandfather and the soldier walked right through the glacier wall in front of them. Mattias stayed where he stood and just watched them. Anna desperately wanted to follow to see what happened next. She threw out her hands and used her power to cut a large hole in the ice wall.

In the distance, the faint sounds of her mother's lullaby filled the air, reminding her that if she went too far into Ahtohallan, she would never be able to return. But Elsa needed to know what had happened in the forest that day. She needed the truth.

She stepped through the hole in the wall that she had created and into a dark, narrow passageway that slowly sloped downward. She walked along it with unsure steps. As her hands rubbed against the wall, memories came alive on it.

"The dam will weaken their lands," her grandfather said to the soldier with him. *"So they'll have to turn to me."*

On the wall ahead, she saw the mighty dam. Many

Northuldra, gathered from far and wide, disappeared down a steep drop at the end of the narrow path. As Elsa approached, echoes from the chamber of memories became more and more distant.

"They will come in celebration, and then we will know their size and strength," her grandfather said.

Elsa stopped at the edge of the drop and looked down, wondering if she should go farther. She saw her grandfather addressing the large group of Northuldra in front of him.

"As you have welcomed us, we welcome you. Our neighbors. Our friends," King Runeard said.

The Northuldra leader stopped him. *"King Runeard, the dam isn't strengthening our waters. It's hurting the forest. It's cutting off the north!"*

King Runeard nodded as if he were listening. As if he were concerned. *"Let's not discuss this here. Let's meet on the fjord. Have tea. Find a solution."*

"Who will stop you from going too far?" the memory of Anna's voice reminded Elsa.

Elsa looked back up the path to the magical light of the chamber of memories, debating whether she should return or move forward. She heard voices coming from it.

"No one really knows what happened that day," someone

said. It was when she'd first met the Northuldra. Then her father: *"For Arendelle's sake."* More voices. *"You're trapped here, too!"* Yelana shouted. *"We've never even seen the real sky,"* Ryder complained. *"A wrong demands resolution,"* said Pabbie. *"Without it . . . I see no future."*

Elsa decided that moving forward was the only choice there ever was. She let her body fall through the darkness until she landed in a forest made of ice. It felt empty and uninviting. It was so cold that Elsa shivered for the first time in her life. The cold had never bothered her before.

She spotted her grandfather walking determinedly through the forest. She started to follow him and noticed Northuldra festivities in a nearby clearing. She moved quickly, searching for her purpose there, the ground freezing around her feet with each step.

Up ahead, she saw the Northuldra leader sitting on the edge of a rock. Elsa was caught by surprise when a snowy image of her grandfather passed through her, heading for the Northuldra leader with a drawn sword in hand. Elsa was horrified by what he was about to do. She reached out to stop him.

"No!" she shouted. She was devastated to see what had really happened in the past, and she wanted to change it more than anything. But she couldn't.

Ice crept up her body, slowly covering it. She panicked and focused on breathing. She tried to use her powers to force the ice off her, but it didn't work.

The ice crept up her neck and toward her face. At that point, she knew she had gone too far, just like her mother's lullaby had warned, and there was no way to return. She gathered all her magic to release in a last-minute signal to Anna. Only one stream of magic escaped, slicing through the air.

"Anna . . . ," she called out desperately. A second later, she was completely encased in ice.

CHAPTER 37

"Which lucky tunnel do we choose?" Olaf asked as he and Anna reached a fork in their path back in the Lost Caverns.

A gust of wind swept across Anna's face, forcing her to close her eyes. It was even strong enough to make Olaf stumble backward.

"Whoa . . . ," Olaf said.

They turned their faces into the wind and witnessed a stream of magic and snow floating on it. Then an ice sculpture formed in front of them.

Olaf stared at it in concern, confused by what it meant. Anna slowly walked around it, examining every detail.

"Elsa's found it," she said.

"What is it?" Olaf asked.

"The truth about the past," Anna answered. It was a sculpture of a man standing with his sword raised over another man, who was sitting. His back was turned to the standing man. The sitting man seemed unaware of the danger as he raised a cup to his lips.

Anna realized who the men were. "That's my grandfather, attacking the Northuldra leader, who wields no weapon." She knew it had to be true—all the ice sculptures they'd encountered had revealed what had really happened in the past. "The dam wasn't a gift of peace. It was a trick."

"That goes against everything Arendelle stands for," Olaf said in shock.

"It does, doesn't it?" Anna agreed. She hung her head as the gravity of the situation took hold. "I know how to free the forest. I know what we have to do to set things right."

"Why do you say that so sadly?" Olaf asked. He thought it was the most exciting he'd heard all year.

Anna slumped on a rock and put her head in her hands. She always did what was best for her people. She'd never thought things would come to this.

"We have to break the dam," she said.

Olaf thought that was the worst idea he'd heard all

year. He thought maybe Anna had been in the caves too long.

"But Arendelle will be flooded!" he said.

Anna had already thought about that, and hated that there was no other way. "That's why everyone was forced out. To protect them from what must be done." They hadn't been forced out of Arendelle because the spirits hated them. They had been forced out so that they could live.

"Oh. . . . Are you okay?" Olaf asked.

Anna wasn't sure that "okay" was the right word. She felt sick to her stomach. "I could really use a bright side, Olaf."

"Um?" He found something that was sure to cheer her up. "Turtles can breathe through their butts. And . . . I see a way out."

Anna smiled. "I knew I could count on you."

Olaf smiled, too. But as Anna turned away from him, he stumbled backward and put a hand to his forehead.

"Come on, Olaf," she said, not noticing he was in distress. "Elsa's probably on her way back right now. We can meet her, and—" Then she saw snow beginning to flurry off her friend and float into the air. Something was very wrong. "Olaf . . . ?"

He looked at the snow flying off his body. "What's this . . . ?" Olaf asked.

"Are you okay?" Anna asked, having no idea what to do to help him. She had a very bad feeling.

Olaf didn't understand why his body was literally floating away piece by piece. "I'm flurrying?" he said. Then larger clumps of snow blew off his body and sailed into the sky. "Wait. That's— That's not it. The magic in me is fading away. I don't think Elsa's okay. . . ." He watched more of his body break apart. "Anna, I think she may have gone too far."

Anna's eyes widened in alarm. "What? No . . . no."

Olaf looked down at his little body, changing with every bit of it that drifted away. He wasn't sure what it meant, but knew one thing: "Anna . . . I'm scared."

Anna was struck by the fear on his face as she began to understand what was going on. If something had happened to Elsa, if Elsa didn't exist anymore, then Olaf couldn't exist. Anna fell to her knees before him, suddenly terrified but trying not to show it.

"No, no, no," she said. "It's okay. It's okay." She pulled Olaf into her arms, holding back tears. "You don't have to be scared. I'm right here."

"Oh, that's good," Olaf said as she held him close. "Remember when you promised not to leave me?" He looked up at her face sadly. "I'm so sorry I forgot to promise not to leave you. You're gonna have to do this next part on your own."

Anna swallowed hard as a single tear slid down her cheek. "You're not leaving me, Olaf. . . . Not ever . . ."

"Hey, Anna," he said weakly, limp in her arms. "I just thought of one thing that's permanent."

"What's that?" she asked.

"Love."

Anna touched her heart. "Warm hugs." She pulled him close and held on tight.

"I like warm hugs," Olaf said, returning her embrace.

Anna choked on a sob, not wanting to accept what was happening to her friend as snow flurries filled the air. "I love you."

Kristoff and Sven approached the ice sculpture of young Iduna saving young Agnarr in the ice garden that Elsa had created after their interaction with the Wind Spirit. As Kristoff watched, all of Elsa's icy imagery flaked away. He held on to Sven, worried about what it meant for Elsa and Anna.

Outside the forest, Elsa's ice palace began to melt. Warm water dripped from the dome ceiling and down the walls into the main room downstairs. The stairs and pillars crumbled into chunks of crushed ice. The magnificent ice chandelier that lit up the whole ground floor fell with a resounding crash. Then the second floor collapsed onto the first floor in a watery splash.

Grand Pabbie stood on the cliff overlooking Arendelle Castle and the village. The townspeople had set up camp behind him, waiting for Elsa and Anna to return with answers. He watched as the icy castle broke apart and floated into the sky. He took a deep breath and hung his head, understanding and fearing what it meant for Elsa. He looked over his shoulder, knowing he needed to tell the villagers the truth about their queen, but he wasn't sure where to begin.

CHAPTER 38

Anna curled up on the cold, wet ground and sobbed. Her heart was broken. How could she go on without her sister? Without Olaf? She had failed them both. Even after Grand Pabbie had warned her to keep Elsa safe, she hadn't. Anna felt hopeless.

It had been a long time since Anna had moved. A cold breeze drifted over her and she shuddered. She had no idea how many hours she had been there. With a deep sigh, she sat up and brushed at the tearstains on her cheeks. She looked around for any sign of hope.

"Olaf, Elsa," she called out, in case somehow they could hear her. "What do I do now?" There was no answer. But Anna hadn't expected one. She knew without a doubt that along with Olaf, her sister was gone.

Anna had seen and felt darkness before, but nothing like what was in the life that lay in front of her. That life felt cold, empty, numb. The life she had always known was gone forever. There was no light left in her world, and she needed to accept her fate.

She had always followed Elsa, but now Elsa had gone to a place she could not find. Anna was overcome with grief, but a tiny voice whispered in her mind that even though she was lost and it was hard for her to feel hope, she still needed to keep going. She couldn't just stop—there was more work to do. Anna simply needed to do the next right thing. And that was break the dam that had been built by her grandfather in hatred.

Anna clutched her satchel to her chest and tried to stand, but she didn't have the strength to even lift herself off the ground. Though she wasn't sure it was worth it without Elsa to guide her, she tried again and stood on her unstable legs by balancing her weight on the cave wall. All she had to do was put one foot in front of the other. If she didn't think about it, if she just kept moving, maybe she could do it.

Anna summoned all the determination she had left in her to begin her climb out of the pit, one step at a time. She couldn't worry about any danger ahead—it was too much to take in. Every step was a choice to keep going. Anna turned her mind to the goal that was bigger than herself. She would focus on that, because thinking about what she had lost was unbearable.

Step after step moved Anna forward and upward. She soon came to a steep cliff. There were only two ways to proceed—by taking a leap of faith off the cliff and hoping she landed on the ground on the other side of a ravine, or by climbing down. Before, she would have taken a breath and a moment of thought, but not today. She had to keep moving forward. She ran to the end of the precipice and jumped as far as she could, landing hard with a thud. Fog surrounded her, so thick that she couldn't see her hands in front of her. But Anna continued forward, refusing to quit.

She soon emerged from the darkness of the caverns and out into the light. Anna shielded her eyes as she walked through the long waving grass on a cliff overlooking the forest. As she looked out, she knew she had to do what no sane person would ever do. She had to destroy one of the only things she had left that she loved—Arendelle. As much as it hurt, it was the right thing to do.

Regaining her strength, Anna climbed down into the fields and walked as fast as she could to the shores of the river. It was the same river she and Olaf had sailed down in their iceboat, where the Earth Giants had been sleeping . . . and still were. Determined, Anna took a deep breath.

"WAKE UP! WAKE UP!" she shouted.

CHAPTER 39

A giant groaned and attempted to stand, clasping his head, disoriented. He couldn't get his bearings and stumbled, crashing onto the other sleeping giants, waking them all up.

Anna's eyes widened as she wondered if her idea had been a good one after all. It had to be—it was the only way for her plan to work.

"That's it," she said. "Come and get me. Come on!"

Another giant slammed his hand down on the riverbank as he pulled himself up onto the mainland, rising to his full monstrous height. His brothers rose after him and rubbed the sleep from their eyes. They all turned to look at Anna and let out bone-rattling roars.

Anna turned and sprinted through the woods as the force of the roar blew her off her feet. "Over here—ahh!" She quickly got up and glanced back to make sure the giants were still coming after her. "That's right! Keep coming! Keep coming!"

She ducked in and out of trees, dodging the massive fists slamming down toward her. One giant threw a massive boulder that landed way too close. She looked at the heavy rock as she kept running.

"That'll work," she said. "This way, guys!"

Mattias and his men stood on a high ridge and watched Anna lead the Earth Giants—who crushed everything in sight—toward them.

"What the—" he said. He didn't know why she would invite such wrath upon them, but he let his eyes follow the path she was leading the giants down. When he realized what she was doing, his heart nearly stopped. "No, no, no, no. She's leading them to the dam!" He raced in that direction with his soldiers following right behind.

Kristoff rode Sven as they meandered through the woods with their heads hanging down, not paying attention to anything around them. But Kristoff's head shot up when he heard thundering booms and caught a glimpse of the Earth Giants lumbering past them through the trees.

Anna burst unexpectedly out of the bushes in front of him, and Kristoff saw the shadow of a giant's foot cast over her. Kristoff spurred Sven on, slipped under the giant's foot as it began to lower, and quickly scooped Anna up. Sven galloped away with them.

"Kristoff!" She couldn't believe he was there, but she had never been so happy to see someone before. She tried to catch her breath. All the running and scrapes and scratches from bushes and tree limbs left her weak and in pain. Yet her heart hurt worse than any physical pain. Her eyes teared up as she looked at him. "Olaf and Elsa—"

"I know," he answered, "I know." He could feel that something bad had happened to them, but he wasn't going to let anything happen to Anna. And she had clearly been running through the shrubbery, pursued by the Earth Giants, with a purpose in mind. "What do you need?"

"To get to the dam!" she said without explanation.

Kristoff couldn't make sense of the situation, but he trusted the woman he loved. The Earth Giants trying to crush them didn't matter. "You got it. I'm here."

"Thank you." Anna held on to Sven's mane as they ran under a canopy of trees, disappearing from the giants for a moment. This allowed the friends to get ahead while the giants blindly searched for them. Sven emerged from under the cover of the brush and galloped up a slope that led to the decades-old dam. Anna saw the dam wasn't in very good shape. She hadn't noticed it the day they'd entered the Enchanted Forest, and this new information lit a flare of hope in her. Now her plan had an even better chance of working.

Sven skidded to a halt when they reached a raised bank of land he was unable to cross.

"Help me up!" Anna said.

Kristoff assisted Sven as he tossed Anna into the air, high enough so she could grab on to the edge of the cliff. Kristoff waited long enough to make sure she had pulled herself up and was safe, then he said, "I'll meet you around!"

Anna nodded and ran for the hill. The dam was so close, and as she lengthened her stride, again hope flashed through her. She could do this. She WOULD do this.

CHAPTER 40

Nothing was going to stop her now. Anna raced toward the dam . . . to find Mattias and his soldiers on guard. She slid to a halt, breathing heavily. "Lieutenant Mattias."

He stood firmly in his spot. "Your Highness, what are you doing?"

"The dam must fall," she advised him. "It's the only way to break the mist and free the forest." Even as Anna said it, she felt her shattered heart crack a little more. But it was the right thing to do, no matter how devastating it felt.

Mattias was conflicted. He felt he could not disobey an order from someone in the royal family, even though the order was in direct opposition to his ultimate directive.

"But we have sworn to protect Arendelle at all costs," he said. His soldiers stood at the ready.

"Arendelle has no future until we make this right," Anna declared. She didn't have enough time to explain everything—the Earth Giants would soon be there. "King Runeard betrayed everyone. He built the dam out of hate. Hate cannot stand. Please, before we lose anyone else."

Mattias took a deep breath as he studied her face and saw her desperation, her weariness. He nodded and banged his sword on his shield. His troop mirrored his action. The soldiers immediately fanned out and made as much noise as they could, shouting and yelling to lure the giants to them.

Mattias and Anna headed for the entrance to the dam. A loud whistle announced a flying boulder coming straight for them. Anna ran forward while Mattias pushed a soldier out of the way to protect him from being smashed.

"Look out!" he called to the others.

The boulder landed, smashing the top of the dam and separating Anna from the soldiers. She was the only one on the actual dam—the soldiers were stranded outside it. She was the only one who could finish the job. Full of renewed energy, she ran out to the center and faced the Earth Giants, who stomped toward her.

"Destroy the dam!" she shouted at them with all her might. "Throw your boulders!"

The giants lobbed huge rocks at her, determined to crush the person who had intruded upon their territory and woken them from their sleep.

"That's it," she said as she raced back to where she had come from.

But one of the giants had great aim, and the colossal stone it threw crashed in front of her, destroying her escape route. She quickly turned and ran in the opposite direction, doing whatever she could to not be an easy target. Boulders continued to crash behind her, and the dam began to splinter. The heavy weight of the water pushed against the weakened spot, aiding in the dam's destruction. Anna struggled to run faster than she had ever run before to outpace the crashing dam and reach the safety of land.

As she felt the ground she was standing on slip beneath her foot, Anna leaped in desperation, her hands grasping for anything.

But there was nothing for her to grab on to, and she felt herself falling . . . until a hand reached out and grabbed her arm just before she vanished forever.

It was Mattias! At first he struggled not to plunge

into the cascading waters that had burst over the dam, and then he was able to brace himself. He held Anna tightly, refusing to let go as Kristoff ran up to him.

"I've got her," Mattias assured him. "Hang on."

"Anna!" Kristoff yelled, terrified to see his love in such danger. He reached around Mattias, and the two of them pulled her up together. Anna melted into Kristoff's embrace, unable to hold back her tears.

But the tears weren't for herself, or for the predicament she had been in. They were for everything she had lost that day . . . Elsa, Olaf, and now her beloved Arendelle.

Mattias slowly got to his feet and brushed off his well-worn uniform. He saw the way Anna gravitated to Kristoff, and how the burly mountain man had done whatever he had to do to save her. Mattias knew without a doubt that they were meant to be together. He put a hand on Kristoff's shoulder. "Hold her tight."

Kristoff was already doing just that. He held Anna as close as he could without hurting her, never wanting to let her go. He kissed her forehead and swore he would never lose her again.

The dam crumbled as raging water tore the rest of it apart and raced into the fjords, making the land around them shake violently.

Across the Dark Sea in Ahtohallan, an immense crack formed in the chunk of ice Elsa was encased in. As the crack spread across the surface of the ice, the chunk took on the form of a large snowflake. Crude representations of each of the elements were etched into every point. And in the snowflake's center, at its heart, lay Elsa.

From the top of the glacier, a symbol of light shot into the sky, illuminating it. The Earth Giants and Bruni, the Fire Spirit, turned and saw the symbol.

With a thunderous CRACK, the ice that held Elsa finally split, and she slipped down into the cold waters below—as the Water Nokk watched.

CHAPTER 41

High up on the cliffs above Arendelle, the villagers, the mountain trolls, and the castle residents wandered about. They talked to one another and tried to remain patient as they waited for Elsa, Anna, and the rest of the group to return from the Enchanted Forest. They wanted to know what had happened in their village.

Then a dull roar filled the air, growing louder with every moment. The people and trolls looked at each other, curious.

"There!" a child shouted.

Some Arendellians screamed and others fell to their knees, seized with dread and devastation as a monstrous wave tore down the fjord without mercy toward their beloved kingdom and homes. Any hope they had of returning to their houses was being ripped apart piece by piece as the raging water shredded every tree in its path and blasted boulders out of the way like they were tiny pebbles. Soon there would be nothing left but memories of the kingdom and the lives they had built there with love.

As the beginning of the tidal wave reached the castle and village, gently pushing at the shoreline before sweeping in with a giant blow . . . the Water Nokk rose from the fjord's depths—and on its back rode Elsa!

Elsa reached out and magically pulled back the wave with the Water Spirit supporting her. She made the water crest and curl back toward the fjord—where its energy dissipated as the water moved away from the village and castle of Arendelle.

The town now safe, the elements that had deserted Arendelle that night not long before swept back into the village. The waterfalls flowed again, wind fluttered the flags, light returned to the lanterns, and the cobblestones became smooth enough to walk on.

On the cliff top, the Arendellians watched in amazement, speechless. Grand Pabbie stepped forward and smiled as he bowed to Elsa.

Elsa acknowledged her longtime friend with a nod. The Water Nokk reared up with Elsa still on its back, spun on its hind feet, then raced up the fjord at great speed, toward where the dam in the Enchanted Forest had once stood.

CHAPTER 42

Anna and Kristoff stood together, holding each other but not speaking. It wasn't the time for words. After the destruction of the dam, they had joined the Arendellian soldiers and gone back to the Northuldra camp.

What came next happened with almost imperceptible slowness. Anna was staring at the edge of the mist, and she realized it had thinned. Now she was able to make out what was on the other side of the fog. And with every moment that passed, the items on the outside looked clearer and clearer, until the impenetrable mist was nothing but a bad memory. She sighed with relief. Anna would have been devastated if she had broken the dam and allowed the destruction of her beloved

Arendelle for nothing. She leaned deeper into Kristoff and he hugged her back.

The Northuldra and the Arendellian soldiers basked in the sudden bright sunlight as the mist cleared all around and above them. They became overwhelmed with emotions as they realized they were no longer stuck in the Enchanted Forest.

Ryder looked up with wonder and amazement at a crystal-blue sky for the first time in his life. "Wow." He turned to Honeymaren. "Look at the sky." They gazed together in awe at the wonderful blueness.

Honeymaren nudged him. "I just didn't realize there was so much of it."

Mattias and Yelana stood together at the edge of the Northuldra camp. "Thirty-four years . . . ," Mattias said.

"Five months . . . ," Yelana continued.

"And twenty-three days . . . ," he finished. They looked at each other with true understanding and compassion for the first time in their long history together. They no longer viewed each other as enemies. And they both thought that perhaps, in time, they could even be friends.

Anna said to Kristoff, "I'm sorry I left you behind. I was just so desperate to protect her."

"I know," Kristoff answered, holding her close. "My love is not fragile."

Even the reindeer noticed that the mist had disappeared. As Anna, Kristoff, Honeymaren, and Ryder watched, the herd of Northuldra reindeer ran out of the forest, weaving through the towering monoliths, still etched with the symbols of the elements, and into a clearing. Together they ran, getting behind one another and looping back on themselves until they'd formed a giant circle. The reindeer grunted and bleated with joy, tossing their heads and nudging each other. The Northuldra children ran after them, laughing and yelling with happiness. Even Sven joined in, not wanting to be left out.

Anna stepped over to a tree that had been half scorched by the Fire Spirit and stood by herself. She needed a few minutes alone as she tried to process everything that had happened in the last day. Everyone around her was overcome with joy, and all she could do was stare at them. How would she ever feel happiness again when deep down she knew Elsa was gone forever?

Gale embraced her, forming diamonds of ice. Anna looked at the diamonds silently. *What are you trying to tell me?* she thought. The Wind Spirit was insistent, so Anna turned and followed Gale to the edge of the fjord, which was no longer brimming with the rushing waters from the broken dam.

Anna saw nothing there—not on the ground, not on the water, not hanging in the air. She heaved a great sigh. Gale swept up some leaves and dangled them in Anna's line of sight, forcing her to look down the fjord toward where Arendelle had been. Something sparkled on top of the water. Anna leaned forward and squinted into the distance. *What is that?* she thought.

At first she thought it was a trick of the water. But the glistening continued to grow, as if it were moving closer to her. Anna blinked quickly, her brain denying what her eyes seemed to see. It couldn't possibly . . . but it was. The Water Nokk glided over the water, majestic and elegant. And riding on top of it was Elsa!

Anna's eyes widened, and she scrambled down the rock ledge as fast as she could. The Water Spirit washed Elsa onto the shore and she stood there—tall, glistening, ethereal. Anna stopped before she reached her sister. It looked like her, but she was different.

"Is it really you?" Anna asked, not sure what to believe, thinking maybe her eyes, or her brain, were playing tricks on her.

Elsa smiled widely as she nodded and held her arms out. "Anna."

Anna rushed to her and hugged her tightly. "I thought I'd lost you!" Tears ran down her face.

"Lost me?" Elsa asked, pushing her sister's hair away from her face. "You saved me . . . again." Anna looked up at her, not knowing exactly what Elsa had meant.

"I did?" she asked.

But Elsa had more to say. "And, Anna—Arendelle did not fall."

Anna was speechless. It took her a few moments before she could ask, "It didn't?" She still wasn't sure that what Elsa was saying was possible. She had seen the water herself, rushing to destroy the village and the castle.

"The spirits all agreed Arendelle deserves to stand . . . with you," Elsa said.

"Me?" Overcome with joy, Anna shook her head softly in wonder.

"You did what was right—for everyone," Elsa explained.

In less than ten minutes, Anna had not only regained her sister, but she had discovered that her beloved Arendelle did not fall, and that somehow *she* was now the queen.

But she couldn't help wondering about Elsa's quest.

"Did you find the fifth spirit?" Anna asked.

Elsa smiled in a way that let Anna know she had found that and more. And then it hit her. Anna had always known that Elsa was special, that she had always been meant for something more, something greater.

"You are the fifth spirit," Anna said. "You're the bridge."

"Well, actually, a bridge has two sides," Elsa said. "And Mother had two daughters." Anna's face brightened. "We did this together. And we'll continue to do this together."

The sisters looked into each other's eyes, and a shared understanding passed between them. Anna was humbled by what Elsa was asking of her, but thrilled to have the opportunity.

"Together," Anna agreed.

"Elsa, you're okay!" the sisters heard Kristoff shout in astonishment. They turned as Kristoff and Sven headed down the slope, excited to see Elsa. She opened her arms, and Kristoff hugged her tightly. He pulled away, feeling slightly out of place. Then he quickly looked her over, confused. "You look different. Did you cut your hair or something?" he asked.

Elsa petted a happy Sven. "Or something," she said. She smiled as Gale swept in around her. "Anna, I need to ask you a question."

"Okay," Anna said.

"Do you want to build a snowman?" Elsa closed

her eyes and focused as Gale swept into the forest, heading northward.

Anna was intrigued by whatever Elsa was up to and wondered exactly what powers she now had. "What are you doing?" she asked.

Elsa smiled sheepishly. She kept her eyes closed and concentrated.

CHAPTER 43

In the forest, water droplets fell from branches both high and low. Before they reached the ground, they turned into snowflakes. More droplets rose from the rivers and the petals of flowers. The Wind Spirit swept across them all, gathering them up in its breeze, making them spin and flutter as they raced across the land, headed south.

Elsa smiled when she sensed she had accomplished something special. The Wind Spirit swept in with the snowflakes.

"Thank goodness water has memory," said Elsa.

Gale released the snowflakes, and they fell from the sky haphazardly. When they began to settle into familiar round shapes, Anna knew exactly what was happening. She rummaged through her satchel and pulled out a beat-up carrot, some well-used sticks, and three very special pieces of coal—all of which she had saved. With a few quick movements, Anna had put them in their rightful places on the snow.

Olaf was back.

The snowman's eyes fluttered open, and he looked at everyone in surprise. "Anna? Elsa? Kristoff and SVEN! You all came back!"

Elsa and Anna hugged him, relieved that their friend was okay. Sven nuzzled him and playfully bit at his carrot. Olaf giggled.

"Oh, I love happy endings," he said with a smile. "I mean, I presume we're done. Or is this putting-us-in-mortal-danger situation gonna be a regular thing?"

Elsa chuckled. "No, we're done."

"Actually, there is one more thing," Kristoff insisted as he turned to Anna and knelt in front of her, pulling the ring from his pocket. "Anna, you are the most extraordinary person I've ever known. I love you with all that I am. Will you marry me?"

"Yes!" Anna cried, and her face collapsed in a teary mess.

Kristoff was overwhelmed with love and admiration for her. He slipped the ring on her finger and swept her into his arms.

Olaf was touched by their love for each other. "I don't know about you guys, but while I still don't know what transformation means, I feel like this forest has really changed us all."

EPILOGUE

A grand celebration took place in Arendelle. Men, women, and children wore warm coats and hats as the last of the autumn leaves fell from the trees. Olaf moved through the crowd, dragging a wagon piled high with books.

"Excuse me," he said to each person he passed. "Coming through."

The librarian, Oddvar, greeted Olaf at an open window when he arrived at the village library. "Morning, Olaf. What can I do for you?"

"I'd like to return these philosophy books, please," he said. "Seeing as I am at peace with the idea of change, and just so happened to have found the meaning of life, I won't be needing them for a while."

"You found the meaning of life," the librarian said, intrigued. "Well, do tell!"

"Oh, sorry," Olaf said, "but each person really needs to find that for him—or herself. Now, do you have any new mystery or romance novels?"

Kai, the royal handler, stood outside the royal tent. Trumpets announced that someone important was approaching. "Presenting Her Majesty . . . Queen Anna of Arendelle."

But when the curtains parted, no one was there.

"When should I go?" said Anna. "Now? Right now? Okay." She peeked around the tent flap at the crowd and then stepped out, nervous and excited.

Her face lit up with gratitude and love when the crowd cheered for her. She greeted each person by name as she passed them. "Mr. Hylton," she said to an older gentleman. "Your teeth." She handed him a napkin with his special present in it. He rewarded her with a toothless smile.

She continued on and spotted Sven, who was wearing a tie. "Sven, don't you look nice," she said, rubbing his head between his antlers. He grunted in thanks.

Someone nearby cleared their throat, and Anna

looked up. "Oh my goodness, Olaf!" she exclaimed. It was the first time she had ever seen the snowman in fancy clothes . . . or really in *any* clothes.

"Charmed, I'm sure," he answered.

Anna laughed with delight. "Charming!"

A familiar voice greeted her. "Your Majesty." Kristoff stood between Olaf and Sven, dressed like royalty. His hair was slicked back in a polished way, making him look far different than the man who had been raised by trolls.

Anna hardly recognized him at first. "Kristoff? Aw, did you boys get all dressed up for me?" she asked.

"It was Sven's idea," Olaf said, while Kristoff fidgeted with the discomfort of his formal wear. "One hour. You get this for one hour."

She ruffled his hair and kissed his cheek. "That's okay—I prefer you in leather anyway." He smiled.

As she continued on to greet the people, Olaf stepped up beside Kristoff to watch the events, now completely naked. "I'm shocked you can last an hour," he admitted. "The things we do for love."

Anna approached the steps where Mattias stood with Halima. He was looking at a square card that he held with astonishment.

"What is this crazy magic called again?" he asked.

"A photograph," Halima said, smiling.

"Photograph. Huh. We look good," Mattias added.

"Halima . . . General Mattias," Anna greeted them. She had been honored to promote Mattias to his new position on her first day as queen.

Mattias snapped to attention, his new uniform brilliant and covered in medals of valor. "Your Majesty," he said.

"Shall we?" she asked him.

He looked down at the biscuits he also held, then handed them to Halima. "I'll be right back," he said. "You can look at our photograph while I'm gone." He chuckled. "I'm just kidding." He kept laughing, like a teenager with a crush.

Mattias extended an arm, which Anna slipped her hand around. He escorted her up the steps to a platform. "How am I doing?" he asked.

"Fantastic," she said.

A curtain covered something large in the center of the platform. Mattias and Anna stood on either side of the curtain. When they were both in their places, Anna nodded, and they pulled the cords. The curtain fell, revealing a bronze sculpture of young Iduna in the wind saving young Agnarr.

The crowd cheered, and Anna couldn't hold back the tears that flooded her eyes.

"Our land and people, now connected by love," she announced to everyone.

Gale swept around her, as if the Wind Spirit were showing approval of the statue as well. "Hi, Gale. You like it? Oh, and do you mind? I've got a message for my sister."

Gale twirled to show it didn't mind. Anna pulled a note out of her pocket that had been cut and folded like a snowflake. Gale pulled the note into one of its currents and swept away.

The note swirled and dipped as it flew across the land. It soared over Arendelle Castle, circled the village, and swept into the Enchanted Forest. It slid from the sky as it neared Elsa, who stood among the trees with Bruni on her shoulder, a smile of contentment curving her lips. Elsa reached up and caught the flying note. She opened it and read the contents.

Charades Friday night. Don't be late. And don't worry, Arendelle's doing just fine. Keep looking after those spirits. I love you.

"I love you too, Sis," Elsa said as she looked up

from the note. "Hey, Gale! We're going for a ride. Want to come?"

Gale flipped around Elsa with a resounding yes, then swept past her to the Water Nokk, which rose out of a nearby stream. Bruni hopped down and headed for the rocks.

"You ready?" Elsa asked her new friend. The Water Nokk stomped its hoof and shook its head yes. Elsa touched its forelock with her power and turned the Water Nokk into a mix of ice and snow. They touched foreheads fondly.

Elsa rode the iced Water Nokk through the trees. She had discovered that by turning it to ice, they were no longer limited to water. Now they could roam wherever their hearts desired.

Elsa passed Honeymaren and Ryder as they herded their reindeer through a field. She waved to them and they waved back.

An Earth Giant woke up and raised the ground beneath Elsa. She and the Water Nokk expertly jumped over the giant and continued on their journey.

The Fire Spirit ran through the trees, eagerly lapping up the snowflakes Elsa created for it. She formed a snow pile for Bruni to jump into.

Elsa and the iced Water Nokk broke through the

line of trees at the edge of the forest and rode across the frozen sea, heading toward the horizon. The Snow Queen turned her face to the sky and smiled. Elsa was exactly where she was meant to be . . . totally free and in her element.